Amalie's Story

Julie McDonald

Sutherland Publishing
Sutherland Printing Co., Inc.
Montezuma, Iowa 50171

vi

ISBN 0-930942-08-6
Library of Congress Catalog Card Number: 71-128605
Manufactured in the United States of America
by Sutherland Printing Company, Inc.

For my mother,
Myrtle Faurschou Jensen Petersen,
and in memory of her mother,
who inspired the story of Amalie Jorgen

To Meet Queens

To meet Queens, go to forests.
Or, more exact, find yourself walking

in a high green Danish wood
of elms, of slim green-shaded elms

the delicate pallor of fish,
find yourself in this elegant

underwater-seeming Danish wood,
and there the Queens will come

to you, will touch
your tired forehead with white hands,

that head which is so tired,
with their white hands.

Michael Dennis Browne

PART ONE

A Tale of Beginnings

1

I was born in the reign of Frederick VII of Denmark. In fact, the King and I shared the same birthday, October 6, and I was named Amalie after his queen, Caroline Amalie.

Danish women have been allowed to choose their own husbands since Viking times, and my mother, Bodil Ormstrup, was no exception. She fell in love with a peddler. Knowing that he met girls by the score as he carried his goods from place to place, she insured her niche in his memory by stitching her name on a cherry-colored ribbon and slipping it into his pack. The Ormstrups were not pleased when Bodil pulled Niels Ibsen back to her with that ribbon, but they respected her choice.

Bodil knew that the ribbon had done its work long before Niels Ibsen returned to her village. On Twelfth Night she followed the prescribed ritual of walking backward to her bed and throwing her shoe over her left shoulder as she prayed to the Three Holy Kings: "Whose table must I set? Whose bed must I spread? Whose name must I bear? Whose bride must I be?"

For a long time she could not sleep for excitement, but as

she slipped over the blurred line between waking and sleeping, she saw a man coming toward her down a long, winding path. Her heart jarred against her ribs as she strained to recognize a face she could not see clearly. The man swung a pack down from his shoulders and dropped it beside the road, running to meet her unencumbered. Niels Ibsen's face was red-brown from a summer of walking from village to village with his wares. His eyes were blue as the Sound and full of love for her. The two did not touch in the dream, but when Bodil woke, she knew they soon would. She had faith in the Twelfth Night formula, for no girl ever dreamed of any but her own true husband on that night.

Looking at a picture taken in my mother's girlhood, I have been certain that my father would have come back to her with or without the cherry-red ribbon, but the women of our family leave as little as possible to chance. Bodil's wide-spaced eyes were big and round with a look of merry wonder. Her lips were full, and her only stern feature was the straight nose that she had from her father, Henrik Ormstrup. Her waist was tiny, flaring to generous hips, and an embroidered shawl's crossed ends hugged a promising breast and a tidy rib cage. Her hair could only be guessed at, for she wore a bonnet with white side puffs showing only two pale, glossy wings pulled tightly from a center part. She was considered a beauty in her village.

Niels Ibsen was nothing to look at. He carried one shoulder a little lower than the other, even when his pack was put aside. His legs were very long, but when he sat in a chair he was no taller than a young boy. In the summer, he was swarthy as a gypsy from the heath, and his pale blue eyes seemed to leap from the dark face as a chimneysweep's do.

Why, then, did she love him? Because he carried the whole world in his pack; amber washed to our shores from southern forests, laces from Belgium that carried an excitement absent from our own Tønder lace, ribbons and gold braid from Paris, glass beads from Venice. His wares were pretty but forgettable. The tales he attached to them were what lingered in a house when he was gone.

"A long-dead tree has wept this tear for you," he would say, carefully placing a lozenge of amber in a young girl's palm, "a great pine that lived in the time of Thor and Odin. How the sea has shaped and smoothed it for your skin! Now for the chain. Perhaps the artisans of Amsterdam can serve you—their fingers are delicate and . . . ah, perfect!"

Bodil married her man of the world, and I was born at a decent interval. I was taken from my parents when I was less than two, and here is the fairy tale that was used to explain the circumstances to me. Must we have fairy tales to make reality bearable? My Uncle Karsten must have thought so. He told me this one.

He and his sister Bodil were very close when they were growing up. While tending the sheep together, they would talk and dream of the future, leaning against newly cut peat stacked in the shape of African huts.

Bodil filled her lap with daisies and wild carnations to weave into a crown while she spoke of a husband and a house filled with laughing children.

Karsten was more interested in sailing and ships, but he agreed that it would be pleasant to have a wife and children in port.

Uncle Karsten (though I never called him that) would hold me on his lap and tell this story about himself and my mother as if they were two other people he had known. He had a good lap. His thighs were round and padded, and they closed completely to make a secure resting place for me. He spoke so close to my ear that his tobacco breath stirred the tendrils

of hair that escaped my tight braids, and I breathed shallow-
ly to avoid missing a single word.

One day Karsten saw a lovely girl. She was Maren Borris,
who had lived in the village always. They had known and
greeted each other since childhood, but on this day she
raised her eyes to his and they saw each other in a new way.
They were the first to see the storks returning from Egypt on
that April day, and everyone knows that the man who sees
the father stork and the woman who sees the mother stork as
they come back to their cartwheel nest—these two are fated
to love each other.

Overwhelmed by his new obsession with Maren, Karsten no
longer heard the crashing of the sea and the groaning call of
ship's timbers. His horizons pulled in to the small triangle
which Maren's feet traced between her father's farm, the
village, and the step-gabled church.

He carved a *manglebroedt*, the traditional courting gift,
which was a wooden rolling pin for squeezing the water out of
clothes. Its handle was a horse in full gallop with the wind in
its mane, and Maren's name was carved in bold, beautiful letters along its two-foot length.

On the day when the pastor donned his fat neck ruff and
long gown to perform their marriage ceremony, Karsten said,
"I could never wish for more than I have today!"

"Don't tempt fate!" Maren gasped, stopping his lips with
her fingers, which he kissed.

While the vows were being spoken, one guest stood outside
the church, clearly outlined in the sunny square of the open
door. Karsten's head turned as by command, and when he
saw the still form of Hansine, a half-witted girl who lived out
on the heath, he scowled and tightened his fingers over
Maren's. What was over was over.

Karsten and Maren moved into a pretty half-timbered cottage on her father's land. Maren's calm beauty grew riper as

she cared for house and husband, and Valdemar Borris found a ready pupil in a son-in-law eager to learn the management of the farms.

At this point in the story, Karsten's voice would shift to a hushed minor. "But there was one thing they did not have—something dearer than comfort or gold—a child of their own." I would sit straighter on his lap, knowing that my own part in the tale was coming.

Bodil had not yet met her peddler, and she often visited her brother and his wife for a week or two at a time. One summer night Karsten asked her to come for a walk with him. Bodil turned toward Maren, thinking to ask her to join them, but Karsten shook his head, and they went out, leaving the wife in her kitchen.

Bodil did not take her brother's arm as she usually did when they walked, and he asked, "Are you cross with me?"

"It was unkind of you to leave Maren behind."

"It would be more unkind to make her listen to what boils up in me and must be said!"

"What on earth could that be?"

Walking ahead of her through the light, warm summer night, Karsten searched for words. A cuckoo called and the hollyhocks were dusky jewels against the walls of the cottage. The scent of the elder was strong in the air.

Bodil seemed to dismiss his urgency, rising on her toes to stretch her arms to the soft mauve sky and exult, "I love summer!"

"Summer or winter, what does it matter when you can't have what you want most?" Karsten cried. "We have no children, Bodil!"

She gave him a tiny push, mocking his self-pity. "If that's all you lack, Karsten, I'll have a dozen and give you one or two!"

"Promise me that!" He clutched her arm so tightly that he felt the shape of the bones beneath the rounded flesh.

Pulling herself free, she laughed. "I promise! Now, let's go back to Maren. She knows the Hedebo stitch, and I want her help with the cap I'm embroidering."

With Bodil's promise secured, Karsten and Maren worked hard to improve their circumstances. Karsten borrowed money from Valdemar Borris to open a store in the village of Ausig twenty miles away. After a modest beginning, it flourished beyond their hopes.

When Karsten and Maren heard that Bodil was marrying a peddler, they feared for the quality of the promised child, but their impatience outweighed their doubts, and they traveled home for the wedding with great exuberance and hope.

Noticing Karsten's close inspection of her bridegroom, Bodil teased, "Would you like to see his teeth? You act like a buyer at a horse fair!"

"Surely you know why I look at him so closely?"

"If you look forever, you will never see what I see!" she said, laughing.

Karsten placed a muslin bag fat with seeds in her hands. "Maren and I follow the custom of Amager with this token of a bright, happy future—and the hope for many children."

"Seed?" laughed Bodil. "The Dutch of Amager are strange folk! I would prefer a bolt of fine linen."

"We have brought that too," Maren said with a slow smile, "But you must honor us by accepting this small gift as well."

Karsten and Maren walked to the long tables heaped with joints of ham, smoked legs of mutton, and prune tarts big as storks' nests. The first notes of the violins were sounding, and they watched approvingly as Niels Ibsen plucked the bag of seed from Bodil's hands and tossed it into a corner, then whirled her into a dance so breathless that her bridal wreath of myrtle nearly fell over her eyes.

"He is lively and she loves him," Karsten said.

Maren nodded happily. "It won't be long."

But it was three years before Karsten came to the home village again. Maren persuaded him to wait until the baby had a strong start in life before taking her from her mother. When the child was just beginning to walk and Bodil was pregnant with the next, Karsten made the all-important journey.

He arrived at night, for it took most of a day to drive from Ausig, and he took a room at the inn in the village. Though he knew that his sleeping under a strange roof would offend his sister, he couldn't risk being with her long enough to let her dissuade him from his intention.

In the morning he put on his shining Hessian boots and the green velvet coat with big silver buttons. He picked up his hat, then tossed it aside, not wanting Bodil to think he was putting on airs.

Harnessing his horse, he drove to Niels Ibsen's house and was shocked at the poorness of the home the peddler had provided for his sister. Without knocking, he flung the door open and looked straight into the face of Bodil.

She sat very still, hands folded over the vigorous movement of the unborn child.

"Well, Bodil, you look splendid!"

"Why did you spend the night under a strange roof? And where is Maren?"

Karsten saw that they were not alone. An ancient village gossip, whom everyone called Lillemor, was listening with keen interest, dipping almond *kager* in her coffee. Niels Ibsen stood at the hearth, filling his porcelain pipe.

"Lillemor, can you not come back another time?" Karsten said. "We have family business to attend to."

Reluctantly the old woman tied the ribbons of her cap and scuttled off to pass along the little that she knew. Karsten's fine and prosperous dress was enough to give her tongue a workout until she could wring something more from Bodil.

"Will your husband stay, Bodil?" Karsten asked.

"Why should he not?"

"Have you told him of your promise to me?"

Bodil looked bewildered. Then, as she started to understand, she swept up the toddler who was pulling at her skirts and held her so tightly that she cried in protest.

"A fine, healthy child, Bodil." Karsten touched the little girl's cheek and she howled all the louder. "We will be able to do much for her. My business has prospered and I have bought a ship that sails from Aalborg to the Indies to bring back spices and silks." He looked around the long, low room with its tiny windows and timbered ceiling. The toe of his Hessian boot kicked at the dark earthen floor. "I have built a beautiful house for Maren—and Amalie."

"You wouldn't be so hard," Bodil whispered.

"You promised her."

"If I should have a dozen, I said—there is only Amalie!"

"Not for long. We knew you were with child, or I would not have come. I know it grieves you, but it is best for the girl. She is of my blood, Bodil!"

"And what of mine?" Niels Ibsen cried.

"Be sensible, man. Can you give her what I can?"

"Your stock may be larger than mine, but what do you know of a father's love?"

"More than you do, perhaps. To you, the feeling is as commonplace as the rain and the sun, but fatherly love has been my study. I have practiced it in my heart for years while I waited for this child."

"Bodil," Niels Ibsen said, "though this man is your

brother, I shall take the poker to him!"

"Don't, Ib," she begged, "not if you love me! I gave Karsten such a promise, and what he says is true. Amalie will have a better life than we can give her. Please help me to my bed now, for I feel sick." She rose heavily, leaning on the arms of both men as she made her way to the curtained box bed in the next room. She turned her face to the wall and said, "Take her quickly! But be sure to tell her that she is mine and that I let her go because I wanted the best for her. Promise me that, Karsten!"

He did, of course, for ours is a promise-making family. This leads to sorrow more often than not, and I often consider swearing off promises, but I always go back to them. Promises keep a person striving.

According to Karsten, my parents were resigned to my going away, even glad about it when they had time to recover from the unexpectedness. I believed this for many years, and Karsten was the fairy-tale prince who rescued me from a dark hovel. He told me that I loved him very soon, before his liver-colored horse had carried us halfway to Ausig, and that I slept in perfect confidence, with my head resting on the green velvet joining of his hip and thigh.

We called this "Amalie's Story," and I preferred it to any of H. C. Andersen's tales, which pleased me well enough. Many years passed before I came to hear scraps of another version of it.

Coming to my new home so young, I had no dramatic first impression of Dovedale. Except for an occasional troubled dream, it seemed a place where I had always been. I was taught to call Uncle Karsten "Far" or Father and Aunt Maren "Mor," and I was at home.

The house at Dovedale was big and costly. Far had wanted a roof of rich, plum-colored tile, but Mor insisted that she must live under thatch as she always had, and he let her have her way.

Most of the substantial houses in Ausig had a sky-blue best parlor, but guests at Dovedale followed Hop-Caroline, the lame serving girl, to a drawing room with dark-patterned wallpaper, a richly decorated ceiling, and frescoes over the door.

I never visited this shadowed room alone. I was afraid without Koll, Mor's white Eskimo dog. He went in to sniff the furniture when the company had gone and protected me from the open-mouthed lions carved on the arms of the big, black sofa.

I was the only child anywhere near Dovedale, unless you

counted Hop-Caroline. The sickness that had made her lame also left her somewhat simple-minded, and we were children together. When Mor drove away in her carriage to visit friends, Hop-Caroline would drop her goose-wing duster to play clapping games with me.

Mor kept Hop-Caroline as a charity, for the girl actually contributed very little to the running of the household. (We always called Hop-Caroline a girl, but she must have been older than Mor.) Mor attended to everything herself, moving briskly from room to room with a large ring of keys jingling at her belt. She made decorative molds of sweet butter; fat, round loaves of bread; towering whipped cream cakes; and vats of brown ale. She carded and spun wool, slaughtered and butchered pigs, and boiled linen sheets in a great tub. Her hands were never still, for when the big jobs seemed well under control, she snatched up her knitting needles or embroidery.

"You must watch and learn, Amalie," she would say, and I had my own small knitting needles before I could write my name.

I tried hard to please her, often despairing of satisfying her perfect standards. Mor was not patient.

My deepest disgrace came with the slaughtering of the fall pigs. Mor put on wooden shoes and tucked her skirt in the band of her long apron.

Pushing her sleeves above her elbows, she took a long, sharp knife from the kitchen table and said, "Come, Amalie."

Hop-Caroline put her weight on her short leg, tapping the foot of the longer one with excited anticipation. She loved slaughtering, butchering, and rendering, and she pulled me along as if we were going to a picnic. Though she was a pious Lutheran, Hop-Caroline wore a Thor hammer around her neck and embraced every superstition that came to her ears. On slaughtering day, she was Odin's daughter.

As we passed through the kitchen garden, the sleepy, spicy scent of the herbs had a mildly narcotic effect on my apprehension, but my fears sharpened again as we rounded the barn and saw Arne, the hired man, looping a rope around the back feet of a struggling pig. It was a pink, naked, human-looking pig, and its squeals were piteous.

Hanging the pig upside down from a strong beam, Arne stepped out of the way with a deferential nod to Mor. I saw the flash of her strong white forearm, the sun on the blade, and a gout of fantastically red blood. Hop-Caroline clapped her hands.

Bent double, I vomited until the lining of my stomach seemed to rise in my throat. I saw Mor's look of contempt through watering eyes and heard her say, "Take her away, Hop-Caroline, she is too young."

Weak and chastened, I spent the afternoon with Far, who devoted one day a week to repairing watches and clocks. He delighted in the intricacies of timepieces and sent Arne to all the fairs in the surrounding countryside to collect faulty clocks and watches. In a room set aside for the purpose he would diagnose and repair, charging the owners nothing for what he called his "pleasure."

The uncurtained room held the full light of the sun. Two long trestle tables were spread with dozens of carved clocks, pocket watches like gold onions, and dainty ladies' watches in cases of porcelain or silver. Far's big fingers moved among the tiny parts with incredible delicacy. The squint that held the jeweler's glass to his eye drew one corner of his mouth upward in a crooked smile.

I was not permitted to talk in this room, but I didn't mind. Far's happy absorption, the warm sun, and the many voices of time conspired to set me dreaming. I would harness Koll to

a very small buggy and go to see what lay beyond the far-
thest hill visible from Dovedale. Away from the village and
all the familiar things that forced him to be a common dog,
Koll would speak like the animals in H. C. Andersen's tales.
The black eyes that gleamed in his white-ruffed, wolfish head
were so knowing that I was sure he would have much to say.
Koll might be able to tell me who called to me in my sleep in
a voice I knew but did not know. During these happy imaginings, it was easy to forget that Koll bit me when I disturbed
his sleep and growled when I came too close to his food pan.

The men who came to visit Far were not invited to the
clock room, and they had no liking for the formal sitting
room. They would rest their elbows on the big dining-room
table of Jacobean oak and talk or play poker, furtively claim-
ing their winnings when Mor was not looking. Mor thought
gambling was a sin, but a game of cards without stakes did
not disturb her, and she would pass through the dining room
from time to time to inspect the ale glasses, calling Hop-
Caroline to replenish the ones that were empty.

I was allowed to play quietly in a corner of the dining room
near the long windows when the men came until Mor heard
me chanting a word I had picked up from the chairman of the
Parish Council.

"*Fordømmelse! Fordømmelse!*" I repeated, laughing at the
jarring, comic sound without the faintest notion that I was
shouting "Damnation!"

"Who taught you that?" Mor demanded fiercely.

When I told her, her lips clamped tightly as a well-worked
buttonhole. She left the room quickly, calling, "Karsten, I
must speak to you!"

While they discussed my unsuitable utterance, I continued
to enjoy a singsong repetition of it, and I was completely
bewildered when Mor told me that I was not to go into the

dining room when Far's friends came.

Missing the blue-gray layers of cigar smoke, the rich depth of male laughter, and the mingled smell of cognac and of boots that had passed through the barnyard, I found a hiding place behind the heavy drapes and enjoyed the forbidden company secretly.

As the weeks passed, the atmosphere changed, and with childlike self-importance, I thought my banishment was the cause. The men were more serious when they came, and they seldom played cards. They spoke of the death of King Frederick, the last monarch of the Royal House of Oldenburg. They worried about the discretion of the young King Christian IX. Making myself small behind the curtain, I listened to talk of General de Meza and *Dannevirke;* then of Dybboel and the Austrians and the Prussians, who were "the Devil's own."

When his friends left, Far would wander to his room full of timepieces, but he seemed to have little interest in them. He sat at the trestle table with his head in his hands and stared at the wintry fields outside.

"Are you sick, Far?"

"Mortally sick! Prussia-Austria has swallowed Slesvig, and the necks of Danes are under cruel boots. How long can Denmark survive?"

I didn't know what he was talking about, but I could visualize Arne, Hop-Caroline, Pastor Madsen, even Far and Mor, sprawled on the ground, with heavy boots pressing their faces into the dirt. My own neck hurt to think of it! As for somebody or other swallowing Slesvig, how could this be? Slesvig was a place far away, and it must be too big to swallow.

"Will the Austrians and the Prussians go to Hell?" I asked.

"They have come from Hell!" Far shouted, bulging the

veins in his neck and spraying my face with saliva.

I had never seen him so upset, and I tried to think of a way to comfort him. I had been told of the statue of Holger Danske who slept with his beard growing into a table in a dungeon at Kronborg Castle. When Denmark was in terrible trouble, Holger Danske would rouse himself from his stony sleep and come to her aid.

"Why doesn't somebody go and tell Holger Danske?" I suggested timidly.

Far laughed as if his throat hurt. "Yes, why not? And we can call on Thor and Odin while we're at it!"

"Don't you think Holger Danske would come? Hop-Caroline told me he would if the trouble was bad enough."

"Don't believe everything that simple girl tells you," Far said, patting my head absently. "I must go to Aalborg. *Dronning Dagmar* will be due in port soon. I would like to sail away with her again! I cannot bear to see proud Denmark in this state!"

I looked through the windows, puzzled. "Everything looks the same to me."

"Because you are a child, you are spared much. Forget what I have said and play with Koll or Hop-Caroline. Even the nonsense of a simpleton is better for you than my bitterness! *Farvel,* Amalie."

I couldn't forget what he had said. The thought of boots on the neck and the swallowing of Slesvig gripped me while I helped Mor scrape carrots, while I knitted at a clumsy scarf, and when I lay in my featherbed at night looking at the stars through the small casement window of my room close under the thatch.

Far left for Aalborg in the box carriage with runners, driving an Iceland pony that took to the snow better than the liver-colored thoroughbred, Brand.

We all turned back to the house before he started up the far hill, for it was considered bad luck to watch a loved one out of sight.

"Which way is Kronborg *Slot*, Hop-Caroline?" I asked, as if I didn't care whether she answered or not, knowing this was the best way to get an answer, for she loved to tease.

She pointed vaguely to the southeast and hurried toward the house, blowing her breath in great clouds to show how cold she was.

I waited, kicking at the snow with my high boots, until she and Mor were safely inside. Then I took the wide road to the village. Wishing for Koll's company, I sadly renounced it. If I went to look for him, somebody would question me or hold me back.

Ausig was nearly two miles from Dovedale, and I was so tired when I got there that I hoped Kronborg Castle wasn't much farther. I walked down the one long, straggling street, and when I came to Far's store, I stepped inside, just to get warm. Dorotea Thomsen was busy selling calico, and I slipped behind the stove so she wouldn't see me and ask questions. I didn't want to leave the warmth and the mixed odors of soap, raisins, coffee, and tobacco, but I was in a hurry to reach Holger Danske. The bell above the door tinkled as I went out, and Dorotea called to me, but I didn't answer.

Beyond Ausig the road grew narrower. The sky darkened and it began to snow. The flakes came thicker and faster, clinging to my eyelashes and turning my red coat pink. With the sun hidden, I lost my direction and stumbled into a tiny lane where two men were digging with shovels. One wore big sea boots and the other had on wooden shoes and long, white woollen stockings pulled over his trousers to the knees. Both wore fur caps with flaps tied over their ears, and they looked like wild animals walking upright.

"Which way is Kronborg *Slot*, please?" I asked.

They leaned on their shovels and stared.

"Won't you tell me?" I was tired, half-frozen, and cross.

"*Lille pige,*" said the man in wooden shoes, "little girl, this is no night for visiting castles! Does your mother know where you are?"

"Yes," I lied, "she sent me."

"Then she's a madwoman!" The man in sea boots spat into the snow. "You'd better come with us until the weather lifts." He dropped his shovel to hold out his arms and I ran the other way.

I went on running with the muffled shouts of the men in my ears. Everything got whiter and whiter. The snowflakes seemed to whirl inside my head, and then there was nothing.

I woke in my own featherbed, hot and feverish. Something was holding me down, and I struggled until I realized that Mor was holding one of my hands and Pastor Madsen the other.

If the pastor was here in the night, it meant that death was in the neighborhood. I twisted my head to look at the window to see if the ice maiden was there reaching for me. Hop-Caroline had told me that the ice maiden took shape in the frost on the pane and stretched out her arms to receive the dying. The window was clear, so I sighed and drifted toward sleep as Pastor Madsen prayed over me and climbed back into the pastor's chair suspended in the wagon that drove him home.

Later I learned that Hop-Caroline had opened the casement and scraped the pane with a table knife, and I wondered how much of my recovery was due to praying and how much to paring.

I was well enough to sit up in my blankets by the time Far

returned from Aalborg, and I spread the presents he brought me on the feather puff. There was a necklace of fish eyes iridescent with their retention of underwater mysteries, a length of cloth printed with strange shapes from the faraway islands, and a bag of rock candy.

I gave Far a kiss of thanks, and while my arms were around his neck, he asked, "Why did you run away, Amalie?"

To think that he would misunderstand me so! I swept the presents off the bed and refused to say a word. I never told him that I was going to Holger Danske. I have never told anyone until now.

In spite of my failure to reach the stone warrior, the spirits of everyone around me gradually improved. The men came to play cards again, and they spoke of reclaiming the heath, saying, "What is outwardly lost is inwardly won!"

When I asked Far what they meant, he said the bogs were being dried out and the heather cleared from the moors to make more land for growing things. They were trying to replace Slesvig, which the Austrians and Prussians had swallowed. He took me with him in the cart behind the Iceland pony to watch the laborious breaking of the heath and the planting of small pines in the ground torn from the heath's stranglehold.

I watched an old couple lifting their hoes high and bringing them down on the tough, matted growth with a stoic strength. Their faces were expressionless, as if they were resigned to an unrelieved lifetime of turf breaking.

Then Far told me of the mythical Gefion, who was offered as much of Sweden as she could plow in one night. She turned her sons into oxen and lashed them into plowing a great body of land that came to be called Zealand. The proof of this feat is a Swedish lake shaped just like Zealand.

"We could use some goddesses like that these days," he said; "men move too slowly."

"But we have longer than one night," I said.

"That is not for us to say."

3

When I was nine years old, my real father died. Far told me that we would not attend the funeral because my presence would only deepen Bodil's grief, reviving an old loss to keep the new one company.

I went alone to the village church and sat there trying to feel something. It was November, and the cold inside the church was like death itself. Even in the summer the bare, whitewashed walls were green with damp, and in winter the water in the font froze and the pastor wore mittens in the pulpit.

In the gloomy light I could barely make out the White Christ on His cross, but I was sure that He could see me, and I was embarrassed that I could not squeeze out even one tear for my real father in His presence. The White Christ of Scandinavia is so different from the broken Saviour one sees in American crucifixes. The White Christ exults in His sacrifice with His head thrown back and His powerful hands thrusting upward with the nails, bearing them like a gift. He requires straightforward worship and fair dealing. I approached the altar cross to stand directly beneath His arching feet and confess my inability to manufacture grief.

Believing that He understood, I went out of the church relieved. Pastor Madsen was on his way in, and as we met, he asked if there were workmen inside.

"No, Pastor, I didn't see anyone—"

He frowned. "No time for God's work! The church can crack in two for all they care! You are a good girl to come when there is no service, Amalie; such piety is unusual in the young."

I explained about my real father dying from pneumonia, which he caught while walking from village to village in the fall rain. The pastor himself was coughing, but he leaned down to clasp my shoulder in sympathy.

"You will see him again, Child."

"But I haven't seen him the first time—not that I remember." I wanted to say more, but the pastor had returned to a worried scrutiny of the crack in the wall.

Pastor Madsen had no wife, but otherwise he seemed like other men when he wasn't wearing his ruff and clerical gown. He told jokes, drank ale, and played cards, laughing around the stem of a porcelain pipe. However, when he climbed the stairs to the high pulpit to preach and intone the liturgy, he seemed taller, thinner, and paler, and he had a way of pulling time out in a long, slender thread which I longed to break. Sometimes I felt as if I had gone into the church one day and come out the next.

The Sabbath began officially at noon on Saturday and ended on Sunday after the big meal in the middle of the day. The step-gabled church was as quiet as the neighboring graveyard until Sunday morning, when the carriages rolled up and the horses were tied to the low, iron fence.

The pumping of air over the condensed moisture in the

organ pipes gave the slow hymns a watery quality that suited the undersea green of the light inside the church; sound and light all damply mingled. Stale air and prolonged droning put me into a dizzy trance that lifted only when we sat down to roast pork, red cabbage, rye bread, and Jutland rum pudding, with the guests Mor casually invited after the church services. The food was our means of returning to weekday heartiness, and as we ate, we recovered from the Sabbath as from an illness.

Mor was quick to take up her needle after the meal, having been without it for twenty-four hours. At Dovedale all sewing was put away at noon Saturday, as every Sabbath stitch had to be taken up with the nose in heaven. The moment Far pushed his chair back from the table, she snatched up her embroidery from the sideboard.

Far called for brandy and lit his pipe, addressing the pastor as he puffed. "I hear you have been to Vartov to hear Bishop Grundtvig preach since we saw you last. How did you find him?"

"He looked as old as Holy Canute come to life," Pastor Madsen said, "but there is power in him from beyond himself. In spite of all the unrest he has brought to formal Lutheranism, I cannot help but admire him. He is an inspired madman!"

I had seen pictures of N.F.S. Grundtvig and thought he was an ugly, old troll, but Far said he was right about educating the ordinary people and teaching them the wonderful stories of Denmark's past. It made them better humans.

Far's eyes narrowed and brightened with cheerful malice as he said, "I have been told of Grundtvig's inspiration—" he looked at me—"Amalie, please leave us."

I was accustomed to being ordered out when something unfit for young ears cropped up in the conversation, but I was nearly thirteen now and felt justified in leaving the room noisily, only to sneak back and listen at the door.

Mor scowled disapprovingly as Far told of the young Grundtvig falling in love with the mistress of a country house where he was employed as a tutor.

Far laughed richly. "The lady knew nothing of his passion, but Grundtvig was convinced that he was committing New Testament adultery, and he threw himself into the uplifting of Denmark to escape his besetting sin. There you have Grundtvig's inspiration!"

"The Lord works in unsearchable ways," Pastor Madsen said doubtfully.

Far had had his sport with Grundtvigdianere and jumped to the Home Mission people, saying, "The Indre Missioners won't admit to having bodies. It makes me want to smack their faces and prove that their non-existent flesh can feel pain! There's something wrong with people who call themselves 'We Holy Ones'!"

Mor seemed about to explode, but she only jabbed her needle savagely into the heart of an embroidered flower. Her mood was a disturbing surprise to Far, and he quickly changed the subject, calling me back to the table.

My confirmation was set for the second Sunday in October, a week after my thirteenth birthday, and I thought of it not as a witness to belief, but as a declaration of growing up. Confirmation would mean that I no longer would be sent from the room, whatever the subject. My hair would be put up and my skirts would be put down.

I had said my prayers since infancy and had grown into whatever faith I possessed gradually and painlessly. My confirmation would be just that—repeating to our friends and neighbors what they already knew about me, or thought they knew. Any dark doubts about my relationship with the Deity would remain my secret. It did not occur to me that others might have similar secrets.

The Saturday before my confirmation it rained until Hop-Caroline muttered about "God's Judgment." The storm was a long time coming and fiercer than any I remembered. The edge of the southwestern sky turned blood-red, then pale yellow, darker yellow, and finally blue-black with featherbed clouds that billowed and ruptured over Dovedale.

I threw open my window to lean into the wall of water, and something pagan possessed me. When the lightning speared the fields, when Thor hammered out his thunder, I wanted to shout. Mor frowned at my wild face as she pulled me inside and scolded me for getting my hair wet.

Peeking from under the towel as I dried myself, I saw her looking at me with the expression she wore when she glimpsed the gypsies on the heath—a look that was two parts disapproval and one part fear with a hint of curiosity thrown in for good measure.

She hung my confirmation dress on a wall peg and touched the gold-embroidered border at its hem. Puffing the long sleeves of the bodice and flattening the round lace collar with careful fingers, she said, "I will hear your prayers for the last time tonight, Amalie, tomorrow you will be responsible for your own soul."

I knelt for the childish prayer that was so familiar that it meant no more than the warmth of the featherbed or the steady glow of the beeswax candle beside my bed. The pastor had told me that I must put away childish things. Knowing it was the last time, I nearly wept through the brief, rhyming petition, "Jesus keep me all the night, set my feet in paths of right..."

At the end, I took Mor's hand to ask her forgiveness for everything I had done wrong that day. She had taught me not to let the sun go down without making peace with everyone, and since everyone was not at my bedside, Mor was the stand-in for my entire small world.

On this night I asked forgiveness for my obscure rebellion in the storm, for shouting at Hop-Caroline when she accidentally stuck me with a pin during the last fitting of my confirmation dress, and for telling Hanne Eskildsen that my confirmation presents would be nicer than hers. I watched Mor's face closely to catch the shadowy smile that told me my sins were insignificant, even adorable.

She wouldn't look at me, and as she pried my fingers loose, she said, "We have raised you no better than Koll, and if your soul is blemished, it is our doing!"

"What do you mean?" I cried, "There's nothing wrong with my soul! I'm going to be confirmed tomorrow!"

"I have looked into your eyes, Amalie, and what I see there frightens me."

"What do you see? What?"

"The Devil—he looks out of your eyes, and you must fight him hard!"

"That's not the way Lutherans talk, Mor!"

She smiled then, but it was a terrible smile. "I am glad that you see my difference! After tomorrow, I will tell everyone and stop the lying hypocrisy of my life! Outwardly I have been an orthodox Lutheran, but my heart is with the Indre Mission!" She blew out the candle and stood for a moment in the doorway, her strong face silhouetted by the candles in the hall. I was afraid of her, and when a flash of lightning bathed her features in apocalyptic light, I pulled the covers over my face to escape her burning eyes.

In the morning I thought I had dreamed it all. Mor came

into my room with chocolate and bread with jam as soon as I awoke, and when Far brought my gifts, she smiled while I opened them. Mor's gift was an amber cross to wear around my neck and Far's was an elegant folding fan from Spain. Hop-Caroline had tatted lace to edge a fine, white handkerchief for me.

After Mor and Hop-Caroline helped me dress and put up my hair, I walked very carefully down the stairs, thinking that the new weight of my piled hair was quite uncomfortable. A gold-edged bonnet with ribbons held it all in place, however, and by the time I climbed into the carriage to drive to the church, I was turning my head as easily as ever.

The sun had come out to dry up most of the heavy rain, leaving sparkling pools between the cobbles. The tree trunks were washed to a wet dark brown the color of soaked cinnamon, and the sky was October blue at its heart-tearing best.

Far was happy and proud, shouting his greetings to everyone we passed, "Good day and God help!" He smiled at Mor, who sat beside him in the carriage straight-shouldered and reserved.

Why couldn't she share his bursting joy? What locked her away from the pleasures of living? I remembered then that she had given me an answer the night before, but the chilling thought of the Indre Mission made me try to think of something else.

The service in the church seemed longer than usual, probably because I knew everyone was watching me and couldn't allow myself to drift into dreams. I was tempted to imagine myself small enough to run along the gold serpentines of my skirt border, but I resisted this alluring fancy.

Afterwards, everyone congratulated me, and I walked among the gravestones and markers while Far and Mor talked longer with their friends. I stooped to read the lettering on my favorite scrolled cross. *"Tak for Alt,"* it said. "Thanks for Everything." This was a common inscription that strongly appealed to me. I considered it a pleasant leave-taking.

Feeling a tug at my bonnet strings, I turned to see Birch Sandahl's round face grinning at me. Birch was in my class at the village school, and he always tripped and pushed me.

"Stop that, Birch Sandahl!" I pulled the ribbons from his fingers angrily.

He caught my wrists and planted a wet kiss on my mouth. "How do you like my confirmation gift, Amalie?"

I scrubbed at my lips with Hop-Caroline's gift, and, seeing nothing in his hands, gathered his meaning. Boys were worse than pigs! If that was a kiss, I might go with Mor to the Indre Mission and give up kissing forever!

"You're pretty with your hair up, Amalie," Birch said, and I relented a little, enough to dance with him after the big dinner party at Dovedale.

There was soup with fishballs, pickled pork, ham, sausages, goose liver pie, layered cake with cream and custard, and thickly frosted Vienna pastries. Bavarian beer was served instead of Mor's ale, and most of the men drank too much of it. I never had seen Far so happy, and I seldom did again. The next day, as she had promised, Mor stopped being a hypocrite and made everybody miserable.

She became a regular Berngerd. That is the Danish way of describing a hard woman, and it goes back to the Portuguese Princess Berengaria, who was the second wife of Valdemar the Victorious. Her name, changed to Berngerd in Danish, means "the bear's keeper." Berngerd was noted both for her beauty and for her harshness.

It hurt me to hear the gossips of Ausig call Mor "Herr

Shipowner Ormstrup's Berngerd," but as I tried to endure the new austerity at Dovedale, I could see some justice in it.

Each day brought a new harangue about a formerly innocent pleasure. The brew house stood empty and unused, Far's card-playing friends were no longer welcome, and Pastor Madsen was not invited to our table. I doubt that he minded, for the whipped cream cakes were a thing of the past, and the fare was the plainest fish or *frikadeller* and pumpernickel.

The sitting room draperies were pulled aside to mortify Mor's pride in her oriental carpet. The unworldly feet of the "Holy Ones" tracked mud across it, and Mor seemed to take pleasure in its ruin.

Our orthodox friends reacted to her fanaticism by lifting their eyebrows and murmuring, *"Jo ja!"* but Far, Hop-Caroline, and I had to live with her, and we didn't know how to respond to her sharp-tongued preachments.

Mor's constant talk of the love of Christ was strangely coupled with cruelty. At least it seemed cruel to me that she would pour cold water into the soup to prevent our "worldly enjoyment" of it.

4

As Mor slipped further into the insubstantial world of the
Holy Ones, Far and I grew closer to each other than we had
ever been. One day when Mor's scolding had reduced me to a
fit of nervous tears, he found me in the kitchen garden and
promised he would take me with him on his next trip to
Aalborg.

"You must see something of the world, Amalie," he said;
"Ausig isn't all of it."

"But will Mor let me go?"

"Do you hear the villagers calling me 'Maren?' And is she
'Karsten' to them?"

I shook my head, thinking that Far never would bear that
mark of the dominated husband, the switching of names.
Lauritz Pedersen in the village was called "Nikoline" because
his buxom wife from South Jutland took the part of
"Lauritz," telling him when to come and go or when to sit
and stand, but Far was still master of Dovedale.

The prospect of going beyond the far hill filled me with nervous anticipation. Eager as I was to see the city, I was unwilling to be mocked as a country girl in unsuitable dress.

Though I never had been out of Ausig, I had a strong sense of its remoteness. A Copenhagen cousin of the Rasmussens had made a recent visit, overwhelming us with filmy morning dresses and green satin with white lace for afternoon calling. A black dress printed with golden lilies fashioned with sleeves slashed from wrist to elbow inspired Mor to deliver a tirade on "heathen display," but I found the gown very beautiful, and my homespun dresses with their touches of red seemed clumsy and peasant-like by comparison.

Still, I did not want to be disloyal to my favorite red and was grateful to the long-ago Valdemar for preserving my right to wear it. Queen Berngerd loved red so well that she asked her husband to pass a law to the effect that she alone could wear the color, but Valdemar took pity on the women of Denmark and refused. I'm sure he suffered for it, poor man!

Far warned me not to trouble Mor about my wardrobe and promised that we would go shopping in the city.

The rumpled red roofs of Aalborg filled me with amazement. They were so close together that I wondered how the people who lived under them could breathe. I wondered too how Brand could trot calmly along the noisy, cobbled streets jammed with carriages and people jostling each other as they rushed along. I thought of Brand as an Ausig horse, and his experience of the city surprised me. I wished that I were as confident.

Far pointed out the Limfjord, promising me some of its famous oysters as soon as he conducted his business at the shipping office near the wharf. When he left me to go inside, he warned me not to speak to strangers passing the carriage.

"They might steal you," he said, laughing.

I doubted that, but as I watched him through the window shaking hands all around with the men behind a high counter, I hoped he would hurry. The strangeness all around made me uneasy, and I drew quivering breaths of the raw, fishy air as I listened to the hoarse cries of the mussel sellers.

A dirty-looking woman as old as Mor stepped out of a doorway to pull at the arm of a passing sailor.

"Ha, Bedstemor!" he said. "The likes of you should do business at night when it is too dark to see!"

She whined something that I couldn't hear, and when he shook her hand from his arm, her face contorted with fury. Pointing to me, she shrieked, "That's what you want, is it? What does she know but butter and eggs?"

"We'll see, Bedstemor, we'll see!" The sailor gave me a smile more infuriating than Birch Sandahl's and started toward the carriage.

The carriage whip never left its holder when Far drove because Brand was sensitive to voice commands and a light touch of the reins. It was tight in its socket, but I pulled it free, and when the sailor was even with Brand's front feet, I flicked the shining, liver-colored hindquarters. Brand reared with a startled whinny, knocking the sailor flat on the slimy cobbles.

The woman laughed, screeching like a rusty pump handle, "You'll do no business with that one!"

The sailor pushed up on his elbows and cursed. His little cap was muddied and crushed beneath Brand's hooves.

Far heard the commotion and ran out of the shipping office followed by a huge, bearded man in a billed hat.

"What is it, Amalie?" He sprang into the carriage beside me and ran his hands over me distractedly as if looking for broken bones while the big man sent the sailor on his way with a rough shove.

"I'm sorry that I hit Brand," I said, "but I could not lay a whip across a man's face!"

"It was the quick way of asking Brand to take care of

you," Far consoled. "I am the one who should be whipped! I shouldn't have left you out here alone, but Maren told me not to take you to places where foul-talking men were gathered."

"*Fra asken i ilden,*" I laughed. "Out of the ashes into the fire!"

Then I jumped down to stroke Brand's soft nose in apology. He snorted faintly and drooled on my sleeve as if he understood. H. C. Andersen would have given him a small speech for the occasion.

"Amalie, may I present my good friend, Mads Hagen, captain of *Dronning Dagmar?*"

Mads Hagen pulled off his hat and held it over his chest. I extended my hand and lost it in his huge grasp as I made a quick curtsey.

"You have had a poor introduction to Aalborg, Frøken Nielsen. If that sailor were from the *Dagmar*, he would spend his shore time in the hold!"

I saw that I was still clutching the whip in my left hand and blushed as I tossed it onto the carriage floor. "May I see your ship, Captain? I have heard about it for so long!"

"Of course, and afterwards Fru Hagen will be honored to offer you *middag* in our house."

The gangway shook under our feet, but I felt quite safe between Far and the Captain. I gazed upward at the three masts, peered down into the black hole of the engine room, and admired the Captain's cabin, which was cozy as a child's playhouse.

On the lower deck I saw a tiny monkey tied to a post. The Captain warned me not to touch it because it bit strangers, but while he was speaking, the monkey bounded to my shoulder and probed my ear with saucy curiosity.

"Well," Hagen laughed, "so Kani does not think you are a stranger! Fru Hagen is the only woman he can abide."

As we left the *Dagmar,* Far promised we would meet the Captain at his home in half an hour.

"Why didn't he come with us?" I asked.

"Because I wanted the chance to tell you about Fru Hagen before you meet. She is a woman of color from the Pacific Islands, where Captain Hagen sailed before he took the *Dagmar.* I don't want you staring like a cod when you see her!"

"I wouldn't! I have seen so many new things today that one more would scarcely make me gasp!"

He laughed and asked, "What did you think of the *Dagmar?*"

What could I say? I had imagined *Dronning Dagmar* as a great swan, and she turned out to be a pack horse of the seas. "She is much bigger than I thought, and it's wonderful to think of the places she has been!"

All the other houses on the Captain's street had two-faced mirrors outside the windows. These "gossip mirrors" allowed the mistress of the house to watch what was going on in the street without being observed. Fru Hagen had no such mirror. Also, there were no snow-white curtains at the double windows, and the customary ledge of houseplants held huge, fleshy-leaved plants that I never had seen before.

The Captain had arrived before us, and as he ushered us in I realized that this home was unlike any Danish house I had seen. The floor was covered with straw-like mats, and the furnishings consisted chiefly of cushions and a long, low couch covered with a printed throw. A brilliant green parrot with a yellow head perched on a T-shaped stand near the window, free to fly about. The openness of the room was unsettling at first, but when Fru Hagen entered with a majestic, noiseless glide, the harmony of it asserted itself like a discord resolving.

"Welcome," she said simply, not holding out one hand in the Danish manner, but crossing both on her massive breasts and inclining her head. A tube of brightly printed blue cloth covered her from armpit to mid-shin, and she wore a paisley shawl over it for warmth. Her feet and the columns of her legs were bare.

Though I had scorned Far's suggestion that I might stare "like a cod," I must have done just that. Liana Hagen commanded the eye with her tawny-brown skin and her thick, beautiful features. She soon left us to prepare the food, and whatever she was doing was accomplished in complete silence. The unshakable repose of this woman was a new dimension for me.

The Captain brought a folding table and four small chairs from another room, saying, "When there are just the two of us, we eat Tahitian style—on the mats—but Danes like more elevation."

I was disappointed, thinking it would have been exciting to eat a meal in such an outlandish way.

Liana brought a big bowl of rice and pork garnished with green leaves from the exotic plants on the window ledge. With great concentration, she placed it in the exact center of the table and returned to the kitchen for a leaf-fringed tray of fruits that were strange to me.

"From the *Dagmar*," Captain Hagen said, taking a wrinkled, green oval in his hand, "Liana pines for the sun, and I try to bring it to her this way."

"Wouldn't it be better to take her to the sun?" I asked, not realizing my rudeness until the words were out.

Far frowned, but the Captain took no offense. "She was sick and needed a doctor. The best man I knew was here in Aalborg, but when she is entirely well I will take her home again."

After the meal, the men took their brandy and cigars into a room where I was not invited. Left alone with the silent Liana, I panicked. I could think of nothing to say, and manners required polite talk of some kind. Even the parrot was mute, as it had been since we arrived.

Liana looked at me steadily with eyes as black as Koll's. They might have been drawn under their folded lids with a hard-pressed lump of charcoal. Then she smiled so slowly that it was like the sun coming up. I smiled back and took a bite of a piece of fruit that tasted spoiled to me. She must have seen my grimace, for she cupped her golden-rose palm under my chin, and I spat out the pulp without thinking about it. Mor would have been horrified, but Liana merely transferred my rejected mouthful to a leaf she pulled from the tray and sat back serenely. Her dreamlike acquiescence produced a sensation of calm that I have never forgotten. Years later when I heard that Liana had died of tuberculosis contracted in the cold damp of the place where she was meant to recover her health, I wrote to Captain Hagen, telling him how often I had drawn on the peace of that hour with his wife.

He answered my letter, thanking me for appreciating in Liana what he cherished and what the chattering housewives of their Aalborg street could not understand. Scrupulous in his pride, he also told me that Liana was not his wife in the ordinary way. She simply had come to him and stayed with him while he was in the Islands. He had called her Fru Hagen in Aalborg to protect her from spiteful tongues. He would not have my sympathy on false terms, but if I still extended it upon knowing this, he would accept it gratefully. I answered with a single line: *She was your wife*, for I had never met anyone who seemed more married.

But I am getting ahead of myself. After we left Captain Hagen's house, we went to our lodgings, and I spent my first night in a strange bed. My room was nicely appointed with tasseled curtains and a French writing table, but the featherbed smelled musty and the carpet was stained where a chamber pot had overturned. I wasn't sure that my prayer before sleeping would penetrate the alien ceiling that seemed to sway in the shifting light from an odorous fish oil lamp. The featherbed was packed hard, and I supposed it had not been aired and beaten for years. At Dovedale, Hop-Caroline flogged the square puffs from the beds once a week. In the end, I threw the feathers off and slept wrapped in my cloak, not dreaming at all, for the impact of my first day in Aalborg was as strong as the mallet stroke that Arne planted on the forehead of a steer in the slaughter pen.

In the morning I asked Far if he always stayed in these lodgings when he came to Aalborg.

"No," he laughed, "when I am not with a lady, I prefer livelier surroundings, but don't tell Maren!"

Our first stop that morning was a shop that sold dresses, bonnets, and French parasols. I chose a dress of lavender Egyptian cotton with a narrow frill of lace at the neck and cuffs. For once I would outshine the golden-haired Hanne Eskildsen, of whom I was extremely jealous. After I made my choice, Far sent me back to the carriage, saying he would join me as soon as he paid for the dress. He came out with a slender, tubular parcel, which I tore open at once. It was a Parisian umbrella, lavender with a ruffle, and Far was torn between his pleasure in giving it to me and worry about what Mor would say. I knew I would never carry it, for my friends in Ausig would laugh at the presumption, but I would always keep it and love it.

The rest of the day was a goggling pilgrimage for me. We visited in rapid succession the castle of Christian III, the Gothic house of King Hans, and Jens Bang's stone mansion, going on to the next while I was still trying frantically to absorb the last. Far had seen it all before.

Hurrying me out of St. Bartholdy's cathedral on the Limfjord, he said, "All these things are man-made, and while they are grand and impressive, they cannot equal what I will show you tomorrow."

"Nothing can be finer than what I have seen!" I insisted.

The next day we headed north toward Grenen and the Skagen. The smell of the sea so excited Far that I had to run to catch up with him when he dropped Brand's reins and started across the weed-pierced sand to the promontory.

"Land's end!" he shouted above the noise of the waves, pointing to a clashing of white foam. "The Skagen—like fighting stallions!"

The waters of the Skagerak and the Kattegat rushing together, locking fiercely, then falling back for the next foaming charge, could be likened to white-maned horses in combat, but I saw something else in the colliding seas. There was a sadness in the two bodies of water wanting to be one and never managing to join in a peaceful swell. I looked at the Skagen through female eyes and grieved obscurely.

"They say that we Danes have no sublimity!" Far shouted. "Let them stand here and say that!"

I was ready to go back long before he was. The frustrated union of the two seas depressed me, and I was convinced that this feeling proved my lack of sublimity, whatever that was. Did any girl or woman have it, or was my lack personal? Hanne Eskildsen had no sublimity, I was quite sure.

Exhilarated by the Skagen, Far talked briskly as we rode along. After miles with no word from me, he said, "Amalie, let us chat together while we live. When we are dead, we may find ourselves lying beside someone who says nothing!"

"I'm thinking about all I have seen, Far, I can't talk at the same time."

He shrugged cheerfully and began to sing, "The finest wreath is made from the heart of summer..."

Far had a full baritone that made the workers in the fields look up as we passed, and I was embarrassed.

Mor's parents, Valdemar Borris and his wife, Stine, were getting too old to look after themselves entirely, and Far offered to build a small house for them in the trees below the kitchen garden.

Before it was finished, Valdemar died, and Stine moved in with two gray and white cats. I loved the old woman, but I also came to see the cats. They were named Palle and Petrine, and their haughty condescension to my advances made up in a small way for the loss of Koll, who had died of old age and was buried at the border of the flower garden.

Bedstemor Stine's presence at Dovedale had a calming effect on Mor's fanaticism, and the short year she spent with us was a relatively happy one.

"Maren," she would say, "look to your house and family and let the next world take care of itself."

One day I asked Bedstemor how old she was.

She smiled quietly, like a cat in a dairy, and stroked Palle, who sprawled on her knees. "Very old, and I shall be older still. Maybe I will live as long as Christian Jacobsen Drackenberg!"

Always interested in hearing about the people of Stilbjerg, the village of my origin, I asked her about him.

"Oh, I never knew him myself," she said. "He was from Aarhus. Niels Ibsen, your own father, told me of this man who lived 145 years."

"But that's impossible!"

"So Niels Ibsen thought until he looked at the records in Aarhus." Bedstemor tugged at her knitting yarn, cleaving Palle's fur with the taut thread.

"How could anyone live so long?"

She laughed. "By breaking all the rules of healthful living, they say. He liked ale, brandy, and mead, preferably at someone else's expense, and he smoked tons of tobacco. When his bowels were bound up, he swallowed a lead bullet, and he was forever thrashing about with a cane or a sword when anyone annoyed him. Perhaps I should try those things. What do you think?"

We both laughed at the idea, and Bedstemor put her knitting aside and dumped Palle from her lap to put the kettle on for coffee. I would have done it for her, but she cherished the smallest task as proof of her independence.

"They say my real mother has married again," I ventured as we waited for the kettle to boil. "Did you ever know the man?"

"Not well. I saw him in the field as I drove by, but we never talked. His name is Tinus Pedersen. Has Maren told you nothing of him?"

"Nothing. She says it does not concern me."

"Sometimes I do not understand my daughter. Tinus Pedersen has given your mother a safe harbor. He is an honest, quiet man who works hard on his small piece of land, they tell me. Of course he is not Niels Ibsen. A second love is never like the first." She went to the stove, wadding the end of her long apron into a hot pad.

Turning to me, she gasped suddenly and fell forward with the red-hot kettle beneath her chest. Palle and Petrine hissed with fright and jumped on chairs as I lunged forward to raise her, pulling her clear of the smoking streams of hot water.

I screamed for help as I cradled Bedstemor's head in my arms, but by the time Hop-Caroline clumped through the door of the little house, nothing could be done for Stine Borris. Her staring eyes saw nothing, and when I loosened my grasp, her head fell forward like a snapped-off hollyhock bloom.

"She's dead..." I said wonderingly. How could she speak to me of love with one breath and die with the next?

Palle and Petrine rushed out of the house with wild eyes and flattened ears. Hop-Caroline whimpered pieties. When I told her to bring Mor, she collapsed on a chair, and when I decided to go myself, she pulled at my skirt and begged me not to leave her with the dead. When I asked her to help carry Bedstemor to the bed in the next room, she threw her apron over her head and wailed. I managed it alone, but the seemingly frail body was heavy and impossible to handle with the dignity I thought necessary. I locked my arms around the chest and dragged the poor feet in their defenseless-looking button shoes.

Mor was with the Holy Ones in the parlor, and when I burst in without permission, she snapped, "Amalie, what do you mean by this?"

"Bedstemor is dead!"

Mor's face went slack and her hands fell loose in her lap.

"Dear Maren, it is a pity that she was not one of *us*," said a sour-faced woman named Rigmor Skaarup.

Mor seemed not to hear. She stood uncertainly and followed me out of the room to the little house below the garden. She lifted her skirts, walking around the spilled water in the kitchen as if it were barnyard filth. Then she went into the bedroom and closed the door. More than an hour passed before she came out, and when she did, she was quite changed.

"Amalie," she said briskly, "send Arne to bring Karsten and Pastor Madsen from the village. Hop-Caroline, heat scrubbing water."

Pushing up the sleeves of her sober black dress without unfastening the cuffs, she tore two onyx buttons from the cloth. They bounced on the floor as she went into the tiny, sun-filled sitting room.

When I had dispatched Arne, I returned to help Mor take all the furniture out of the sitting room, and when Hop-Caroline staggered in with buckets of hot water, the three of us scrubbed walls, ceiling, and floor.

While the wet surfaces were drying, we washed Bedstemor. We dressed her in her best striped silk, combed her hair, and laid coins on her eyelids.

Clean white sheets were pinned to the walls of the sitting room, and Mor was impatient for Arne to return so the coffin could be brought from the barn and placed on trestles in the center of the room.

When Valdemar Borris died, the carpenter had made two coffins in matching wood and design, saying that while he was not busy at the time, he might be when Stine Borris joined her husband. Bedstemor was pleased with the arrangement. She often strolled to the barn to pull off the coverings and admire the coffin with its angled top and tapered foot. Hers was shinier than Valdemar's, for the carpenter could take more time with the polishing, and the leaf-bordered cross on the lid was carved with more precision than the other had been.

Pastor Madsen, who had not been welcome in our house for several years, looked somewhat apprehensive as Far helped him from the carriage, but Mor went to meet him calmly and offered her hand. They talked quietly in the courtyard while Far and Arne carried the coffin to the little house. When Far beckoned from the door, we all walked down there and filed into the sheet-draped sitting room for prayers. The men had been clumsy in transferring Bedstemor from the bed to the coffin, and Mor wouldn't let the pastor begin until she had arranged Stine Borris' dress and hair.

It was March, and Bedstemor could lie in state for the customary two weeks without the problem that accompanied warm-weather deaths. Not many of the neighbors had known Stine Borris, but they came to call out of respect for Fru Shipowner Ormstrup, stopping at the big house for food afterwards.

I took my turn at receiving callers in the white room every third day. Hanne Eskildsen came one snowy afternoon when I was there.

"Aren't you afraid?" she whispered.

"Why should I be? Bedstemor is the best of company!"

Hanne gasped, putting her fat, pink fingers to her full, pouting mouth. "You shouldn't talk that way!"

"I'll say what I please! She's *my* grandmother!"

"She is not!" Hanne cried. "Fru Ormstrup is not your mother!"

"That's none of your business!" I said, wanting to pull the yellow sausages of her hair. My parentage was not a secret, and I wasn't ashamed of it, but leave it to Hanne to make my situation sould like an inferior arrangement!

She edged closer to the coffin and peered at the sharp profile that thrust upward like a Viking ax. Then her fat hand shot out to touch Bedstemor's nose and fly back as if it had been stung.

"It's as cold as the nose of Tycho Brahe!" she shrieked.

I slapped her, outraged at the liberty she had taken, and when she ran to the big house to tell Mor what I had done, *I* leaned over to touch Bedstemor's nose.

It *was* cold, but surely nothing like the enameled gold and silver nose the great astronomer had fashioned for himself when his real nose was cut off in a duel. He carried a box of glue around with him to keep himself in one piece. Bedstemor would think Hanne's stupid remark was funny if she knew. Maybe she did.

I looked out the window to see Mor coming from the big house, her skirts flying in the high wind. I watched her approach gloomily, thinking that Hanne really had made this a Tycho Brahe's day for me; that was what an unlucky day was called. Brahe had been warned by an astrologer to avoid bad luck, and the day he stayed in his lodging to keep out of trouble, he was visited by a fellow student who quarreled with him and provoked him to the duel that lopped off his nose.

Mor came in shaking the snow from her shawl with an angry snap. "Did you strike Hanne Eskildsen?"

"Yes," I said, telling her why.

She tightened her mouth to keep it from twitching up at the corners. "Very well, you must be punished. Hanne is in the dining room eating whipped cream cake and drinking chocolate. You will sit beside her and eat pumpernickel without butter."

Galling though the prospect was, I nodded. I had expected worse. Mor took my place beside the coffin, and I threw a shawl over my head to run to the big house and get the humiliation over as quickly as possible.

"Amalie," Mor called after me, "Hanne could *use* a slap or two! Let that thought be the butter on your bread."

Hanne was licking her fingers daintily when I came into the

dining room with my meager plate, and she took another piece of cake she really didn't want just to spite me. I ate my dry bread with gusto, enjoying the sight of the dull red mark of my hand on her perfect cheek. Hop-Caroline stood behind Hanne, rolling her eyes to show a sympathy that I really didn't need, and Far slipped me a sugar cube under the skirt of the table cloth.

Mor had made ale for the guests, as well as all the other good things we hadn't seen for a long time, and though we didn't know it then, she was on her way back to the formal Lutheran fold. The Holy Ones had been cold comfort in her time of sorrow, and she turned gratefully to the comfortable rites of Lutheranism which Bedstemor had known and loved.

Stine Borris had the finest curly cross in the graveyard, and it was inscribed with my favorite *"Tak for Alt."*

One day when the broken earth of her grave was healed by growing things, Far and I were laying beech boughs around it.

"Tak for Bedstemor!" I said.

"Amen!" he said fervently.

50

6

Mor's return to orthodox Lutheranism led to a summer of discovery for me. Pastor Madsen had friends in Hjørring whose daughter was to be married on St. Hans' Day, the tenth of November. While they knew that Pastor Madsen's unmarried state prevented him from supplying the customary household training in a country parsonage, they believed he could persuade some worthy family of his parish to train their daughter.

At first Mor was doubtful about the undertaking, but Far argued that it was her Christian and patriotic duty. Allowing city girls to marry without the proper training would weaken the Danish home and family. Actually, I believe he wanted her to have something new to think about, for in spite of her disillusionment with the Holy Ones, she showed signs of missing their endless meetings.

Jette Berntsen arrived in mid-May, flashing trim ankles in shining black silk as she jumped lightly from her father's carriage. Arne and Hop-Caroline carried six large, strap-bound cases into the house while Herr Apothecary Berntsen herded his wife and daughter into the parlor.

I had been trained not to be forward with strangers, so I waited in the dining room until Mor should call me to be introduced. I paced the room, running my hand along the chair backs as I indulged my curiosity about the lively Jette.

We knew nothing about her aside from Pastor Madsen's assurance that he had known her parents from boyhood and they were staunchly devout people. This seemed evident, for Herr Berntsen carried himself with sober dignity and Fru Berntsen was a small, self-effacing woman who seldom raised her eyes. Jette, however, was brown-haired and as rosy of face as if she had been running. Her eyes were bright, round, and dark as newly cut peat.

As Hop-Caroline passed through with a tray of coffee and cakes, I sighed with impatience. The eating and the compliments would take forever!

"Never mind," Hop-Caroline said, "you'll see more of the young miss than you care to before St. Hans' Day!"

The group in the parlor ate, drank, and exchanged pretty speeches for what seemed like hours, but finally Mor rose and offered to show the Berntsens the rest of Dovedale. I was presented to them and given permission to take Jette to the garden.

"There will be time enough for her to learn the house," said Mor, smiling.

As soon as we were outside, Jette said, "Can they see us from the windows?"

"No, Mor will take them to the kitchen first."

She tossed her bonnet on the stone bench at the edge of the graveled walk and unfastened three tiny pearl buttons at her throat. Flinging her arms high in the air, she laughed, "I'd undo my stays too if I dared!"

Her exuberance would be something new for Dovedale, I thought, and while I found it attractive, I felt I should warn her to keep it hidden or it never would survive the months she was to spend with us.

A million questions about Jette herself, Hjørring, and the man she was to marry crowded into my mind, but I was too shy to ask them. Instead, I answered hers about the flowers that grew along the path: St. John's wort, oxeye daisies, forget-me-nots, lady's smocks. It was too early for the blossoms, but Jette said she wanted to know what would bloom where.

"In winter I always imagine summer, and in the fall, I think how spring will look," she explained, narrowing her eyes at the borders of green leaves. "I try to think how I will look when I have been Ernst's wife for ten years—or fifty."

"But if you always think of another time, you miss now," I said, puzzled.

"Why, that's just what Ernst says! He should marry *you*!"

I blushed. "It must be wonderful to think of your wedding day!"

"It isn't at all what they say..."

She looked so sad that I wanted to put my arm around her, but I didn't dare. The others were coming into the garden, and she buttoned her collar quickly, tying the ribbons of her bonnet firmly under her chin.

Fru Berntsen showed more animation in her tearful farewell than she seemed capable of and Jette much less. As soon as we turned our backs on the carriage to avoid watching it out of sight, Mor told Jette to change her fine dress and the schooling would begin.

In the weeks that followed, Mor showed uncommon patience with Jette, who seemed to know nothing about the simplest household tasks. Jette cut away half the potatoes while peeling them, let whipped cream turn to butter, and left triangles of dust in the corners of the floor.

"You must set your mind to what you are doing," Mor would tell her, more gentle than she had ever been with me. "Now I will show you how to knead bread dough."

Mor lifted a great lump of dirty-looking rye flour dough and threw it on the board, folding it over and coming down hard on it with the heels of her palms, then turning it halfway around for another slap, fold, and shove.

Jette tried, poking at the dough with such gentle little pushes that it scarcely showed a dent.

"No, no." Mor motioned Jette aside, but Hop-Caroline called her and she left Jette to me.

I enjoyed kneading dough, and Jette seemed to learn from me more readily. She started to sing, keeping time with the thrusts of her hands. When Hop-Caroline heard this, she clapped her hands to her ears and ran from the kitchen.

"What's the matter with her?" Jette asked.

"It's bad luck to sing while making bread, and you never mix it on Sunday, Monday, or Thursday. Haven't you heard that?"

"Never," Jette laughed, but she stopped singing, and she was delighted to pull her tiny, white hands out of the dough when I told her I would take over the kneading. I was afraid that she would do such a bad job that the loaf would crack, and that meant a death, as everyone knew.

Mor turned a great deal of Jette's training over to me, and while we churned, carded wool, and stirred preserves, she would tell me of her life in Hjørring.

"Two winters ago when I was just your age, I went to wonderful parties," she said, "there were dinners with many courses and wines. We wore full evening dress and sat at table until midnight, talking and making speeches. Then the young people would dance until the sun came up. Sometimes we had evenings of singing and music or we would walk and listen to the nightingale."

"I did not know the people in Hjørring were so fine," I said.

"There are a few. I'm not at all fine, but I was invited because a certain young man wanted me with him."

"Ernst?"

A fleeting look of disgust crossed her face. "Not Ernst! He dances like a beast from the horse fair at Hjallerup!" She poked her tongue out and made a big show of biting it as punishment for the disloyal remark. "Ernst is a good man, though."

"Tell me about the other one. He sounds like a prince!"

"Ah, Amalie, I must not think of him now. That is over, but there was a time when there was such love between us that neither of us knew an hour's peace. At night I would sigh, stretch my arms and legs and try to get out of bed as if someone were calling me. Mikael's longing was strong enough to reach me clear across the town, and he said he felt mine in the same way."

"Then you should have married him."

"It was impossible. As I told you, I am not at all fine, and Mikael is. One of his ancestors was an adviser to Christian IV. We were cut from different cloth, Mikael and I, and we could have been happy nowhere but in the bed of love."

"Isn't that enough?"

"No, Amalie, it is not enough. The day is longer than the night. When I marry Ernst, I can walk as though I deserved my space."

"You are beautiful enough to do that no matter who your husband may be!"

These words of admiration pleased Jette so much that she let me borrow some of her French scent, and Mor raised her eyebrows at my fragrant arrival in the dining room for *middag*.

I learned as much from Jette as she learned from me, perhaps more, for I was more eager to learn what she knew. She told me that her rosy cheeks resulted from painful pinching; that scent was to be applied to the pulses, even the backs of the knees; and that a small curling iron held over flame or a few handkerchiefs stuffed in the bodice would make up for what God forgot. I didn't need the handkerchiefs, but the curling iron was a blessing, for my hair was reed-straight and did nothing to soften my strong features.

"And you must be a little less than honest with men and boys, Amalie," she said. "They invent the women they love, and we must seem to be what they imagine."

"That doesn't seem right, Jette!"

"Right or wrong, it's the way things are!"

I thought about Jette's Mikael a great deal. If I ever met such a man, I would expect him to raise me to the summit of his kind of life by making me his wife. Jette was too willing to settle for less.

When Ernst Spandet came to visit his betrothed, I was shocked that a girl who had known a love like Mikael's could consider marrying this sober, middle-aged dairy farmer.

He was blocky as a prize beef, and his eyes were the chalky pale blue of a faded work shirt, thatched by thick, white-blond eyebrows. When he walked in the garden with Jette, he stayed half a step behind her, mooning over the cascade of brown curls brought forward over her left shoulder. Her polite small talk and forced smiles seemed to affect him like Holy Communion. When Jette excused herself on the pretext of household duties, Ernst would roam the garden with a lost look until Far joined him for a cigar and a passionate discussion of milk and butter yield.

I pulled Jette into the brewhouse and said, "Don't do it, Jette, don't marry him!"

"I have promised. Mor would die of shame if I broke my word now."

"Promises bring nothing but trouble!" I cried. "I'll never make one—never!"

Jette laughed. "The man who gets you will have his hands full!"

As St. John's Eve approached, contentment lay over Ausig and its surrounding lands like a featherbed. The crops were planted and doing well, the storks were tending their awkward young on the rooftops, and the sun was back with us. At Dovedale we had been eating the noon meal out of doors for many days with no rain to mar the pleasure.

"I feel like a rose unfolding!" Jette sighed, bringing a creamcoated strawberry to her lips with a tiny silver spoon.

We talked of the Midsummer celebration, and Mor did not think it proper for Jette to attend the village picnic and then dance for most of the night near the bonfires on the green.

"It would be different if Ernst were here," she said.

"Ernst would not be pleased to think of me sighing in my room on Midsummer's Eve," Jette said with a modest lowering of her thick lashes.

"She may never see Midsummer in the country again," I said emotionally.

Mor's eyebrows shot up. "I suppose Ernst Spandet keeps his cows in Hjørring?"

Even Hop-Caroline dared to put in a word. Clasping her stubby hands ecstatically, she breathed, "But, ma'am, there is no place in the world like Ausig in June!"

Far settled the matter. "Of course she shall go. Amalie will be with her."

Hop-Caroline was told to pack a basket of food, and we hurried upstairs to get ready. I put on the lavender Egyptian cotton Far had bought for me in Aalborg. The bodice was tighter than it had been the last time I wore it. That was for the Pedersen baby's christening, and the child was now at the creeping stage. Mor would consider the fit immodest, but I had nothing else I liked so well, and Jette lent me a lacy shawl to cross over the bodice, at least until we were out of the house.

She wore a dress that I loved; a soft green lawn with a fichu of ruffles. As we passed through the garden, she picked a handful of oxeye daisies to fasten to her hair. She was summer itself and lovely enough to make one gasp.

Arne harnessed the newly broken horse that Brand had sired and drove us to the green, where Birch Sandahl was pelting Hanne Eskildsen with handfuls of grass, making her shriek like a pig. Some of the older boys were walking among the piles of wood laid for fires to frighten away the witches as they flew over on their way to the Harz mountains. The pyramids of wood would be kicked over and rebuilt many times before matches were set to the kindling. Every male on the green thought his way of laying a fire was best, and fights often resulted from such claims.

With her bright cheeks and her pale green dress, Jette did look like a rose. I noticed how Hanne Eskildsen stared at her, too stupid to hide her jealousy.

Arne spread the carriage robe for us at the edge of the beech copse and went off to find his own amusement. Jette suggested that I join in the games, and while I didn't want to leave her alone, I couldn't resist the running tag. I ran well and knew it, not like a girl at all, Far said.

The sheer joy of motion caught me, and soon I was dodging the firewood piles and taking part in a general chase with all the childishness I had scorned earlier. It was summer!

When I returned to Jette, she had unpacked *smørrebrøddet,*

the fruit, and *kagerne,* and we ate in the soft, golden light of the lowering sun.

The singing began in a twilight the color of dark honey. "There is a lovely land that proudly spreads her beeches...," Far's favorite, "The finest wreath is made from the heart of summer..." and the lively *"Sim sala dim sala..."* Jette's high, clear soprano soared above the other voices, silencing me with its beauty.

Then the fires were lit to scare away the witches and the darkness. There was cheering and clapping as each new flame caught and flared. Jette and I watched from a royal distance, spectators at a lively performance until Birch Sandahl approached. He towered above us, kicking at the grass.

"Will you be my *gadelam,* Amalie?"

"Did Hanne turn you down?" I asked haughtily.

Jette laughed. "Don't be cruel, Amalie, do go and dance. I'd love to watch you!"

I went with Birch grudgingly, thinking how Jette would sit alone imagining some other Midsummer's Eve, missing this one. What a waste!

Since the year before when he had stepped on my insteps, Birch had learned to dance well. He swung me high without straining and held the positions of the statue dance as if he were carved from marble.

The fabric of my dress gave and ripped at the armhole, but I didn't care, and it didn't matter that the fringe of hair on my forehead was losing the waves Jette's curling iron had achieved. All my feeling was concentrated in the hand that Birch held for the circle dance. The hand on the other side might have been the branch of a tree for all my awareness of it. I was eager for the parts of the dance that called for close holding and wondered why? I didn't even like Birch!

When we were out of breath, we stepped out of the dance and moved toward the trees, marveling at how the light stayed with us so far into the night. Jette was not where we had left her, and I was worried.

"She is older than you and knows what she is about," Birch said. "Come, let us walk."

I agreed, thinking I would look for Jette as we went along. When Birch took my hand, I let him keep it, and we were deep in the beeches very quickly. Distance softened the music until it was no louder than the tune Jette's French powder box played. We could hear cuckoo calls and the rusty peep of tree frogs. Birch broke off a low-hanging bough to hold behind me like a spread peacock's tail, and we both laughed, turning to look at the faraway bonfires. They were ruddy constellations brought low. Then he kissed me, and I was stunned by the difference between this kiss and the one I had scrubbed away on my confirmation day. My arms reached to hold him without a conscious command, lengthening the rip in my dress, and his lips were at the parting of the cloth.

"I must find Jette—" I said weakly.

"Later—"

We kissed again. I was melted inside, reckless of all consequences, and well on my way to shame in the month of March when a distant tree trunk seemed to move. It was Jette, and she was with someone. I hoped they hadn't seen us as I held my hands over the torn bodice.

But my behavior was the last thing Jette was thinking of. She floated closer with her hand on the man's arm and spoke without taking her eyes from his face.

"I have met an old friend, Amalie; this is Mikael Gyldendal from Hjørring."

He bowed with negligent elegance, showing off the waves

of his yellow hair. "Jette speaks pleasantly of you, Frøken Nielsen."

I presented Birch to this Dresden china courtier and saw how my dancing partner suffered by comparison. Birch's hair was plastered damply to his forehead, his features seemed blunt and coarse, and the hands that had thrilled me in the dance hung down like two shovels. I must have been mad to kiss and want more from this brute!

When Jette pulled me aside for a private word, I whispered, "Why is Mikael here? Is he going to take you away with him?"

"No, I won't let him, but we never really said goodbye, and he says the longest day in the year is best for that. Make some excuse to Arne, put a convincing body of pillows in my bed, and leave the kitchen door unlatched, will you? I want something to remember through all the years."

I did as she asked, thrilled by imaginings of that Midsummer leave-taking, but Jette was her own undoing. She tripped over some sabots Arne had left beside the kitchen door and woke Mor. They had a grim session behind the sliding doors of the parlor, and Jette was sent back to Hjørring the next day.

Later I heard that Jette did not marry Ernst Spandet on St. Hans' Day or at any other time. She opened a lace shop in Hjørring and lived in the back rooms, where Mikael Gyldendal was said to visit her when he could.

Believing that Jette had been a bad influence on me, Mor spent the rest of the summer lecturing me on pride and purity. It was very tiresome, and I blotted it out with memories of Jette as I fondled the bottle of French scent she had given me on the morning of her tearful farewell.

I languished through the August rains, bored without my friend and filled with questions I hadn't thought to ask until her swift departure raised them. What were these secret dreams of the blood? What was this song of the senses? The first time I saw the sculpture of Kaj Nielsen, which was much later, a wordless answer came to me. Nielsen's sensual, fertile women told the mystery of the flesh in stone.

There were glowing mysteries and dark mysteries, and the late summer brought one of the darkest. Arne, who had been with us as long as I could remember, was dismissed and pushed into the road to Ausig with no time to collect his belongings.

I heard Far shouting in the barn; saw him lay hands on Arne, who was much the bigger of the two; saw the tight, white ring around Far's lips as he danced Arne's slack form toward the road.

"Come away from the window," Hop-Caroline begged.

"But what's wrong? What happened?"

"Nothing for you to know."

"If you don't tell me, I'll ravel your tatting!" I said cruelly, snatching at the bobbin that peeked from her apron pocket.

The threat carried no force, for Hop-Caroline's tatting never grew beyond a misshapen spiderweb, and she was dying to tell what she knew.

"You must never tell Fru Ormstrup," she cautioned, popping her beady, blue eyes.

"May the three-legged hell horse carry me away if I tell!" I promised impatiently, leaning close to hear her whispering. The odor from her bad teeth was sickening, and I hoped the revelation would be brief.

"Herr Ormstrup finally found out what Arne does with Gyda!"

"He milks her twice a day, even *I* know that!" I said, disappointed. Gyda was Far's prize black and white milk cow, a holstein he had brought from South Jutland. I started to walk away, thinking Hop-Caroline was growing more simple-minded every day.

"I knew Arne would be caught," she said triumphantly, "and the fool thought he was safe because the beast is dumb!"

"Does he beat Gyda? No wonder Far was angry!"

"Only when she won't stand still for him. Many's the time I've watched him climb up on that box and—"

I put my hand over her mouth, denying the confirmation of what I was thinking. Arne had lifted me into the carriage when I was too little to reach the step. I had sat beside him while he ate his meals in the kitchen, watching him chew with slow deliberation. I had seen him bending over the plow handles until the back of his neck was deep red from the sun. I knew that he had lifted Bedstemor Stine into her coffin. Knowing all these things, I did not know Arne, and the sudden strangeness of him unsettled me as much as the thing he had done.

Dazed, I went to the barn and stared at Gyda, who was tied in her stall. She chewed placidly, oats spilling wetly from her mouth. For an instant, I saw Arne with coffee-soaked pumpernickel dropping from the corners of his mouth; lonely, silent Arne. Disgust and pity battled within me until I felt ill.

Arne hid in barns for a week, and then the Pedersens found him hanging from a beam above their sheep. Far ordered the coffin and hired two men to dig Arne's grave outside the fence of the burial ground in a place reserved for those who had taken their own lives. The grave was left unmarked, and the mention of Arne's name was forbidden at Dovedale.

7

When I finished my studies at the village school, I was restless. The other girls were busy filling their dower chests, but I had no matrimonial prospects, and all that sewing in behalf of an unknown future husband seemed pointless.

After I finished the many household tasks Mor set for me, there was still time to fill. I walked, dreamed, and read.

Pastor Madsen gave me permission to spend as long as I liked in his personal library, but after one visit to the book-choked room in the parsonage, I decided that his theological tomes were of no interest to me.

Far suggested that I send to Copenhagen for books, naming a shop he knew. Having little background for choice, I put myself in the bookseller's hands, and he mailed me Jens P. Jacobsen's *Fru Marie Grubbe*.

No woman I knew would admit to being anything at all like Marie, but I recognized some of her qualities as my own. Marie would look out a window and want to throw herself down from it, merely to be taking action. She would stare at her bare, blue-veined arm and bite it or put a cold knife blade down her back just for the sensation. Marie was tethered below the threshold of her capacities, and in the fighting of a battle she didn't understand, she destroyed herself; or so it seemed to me.

I tried to discuss the book with Far and succeeded only in frightening him about the unhealthy tendency of my thinking. As a result, he sent me to Sandinge Folk High School to regain my perspective.

Sandinge was one of Grundtvig's "schools for life" where there were no exams or degrees, and where anyone who wanted to learn was welcome. Boys attended in the winter when farm work lessened, and girls were there in the summer months.

The main building was red brick covered with ivy and honeysuckle. It looked like an old castle, and the lecture room might have been an old Norse hall with its paneled ceiling and carved heads.

Sandinge rang with the words of Danes in love with learning. We absorbed history, literature, language, ancient chronicles and sagas, mythology, psychology, and science. We learned through listening, for academic aridity was anathema to Grundtvigdianere, and lively presentation was all.

Lively it was. The lecturer who told us how Shakespeare had found his Hamlet in the ancient chronicles of Saxo Grammaticus swung an imaginary sword as he explained that the original Amleth, a minor noble, was a bloodier fellow than the bard's prince. Instead of stabbing Polonius behind the arras, Amleth chopped his man to pieces beneath the straw on the floor and fed the remains to the pigs. Making this deed sickeningly vivid, the lecturer went on to describe how Amleth invited his foes to a feast, locked them in the house while they were carousing, and set the place afire. We could almost hear the screams of the roasting guests.

Legends and factual history were woven together in the Greek manner, and we were taught how one grew from the other. Though Bishop Grundtvig had devoted his life to proving the centrality of Christ in world history, we were expected to learn about the pre-Christian worship of Thor and Odin. We found much to praise in this layman's religion practiced by high-hearted men not overburdened with brains or troubled about their souls. It reflected manliness, generosity, loyalty, friendship, and a certain rough honesty—not a bad set of values for the Norsemen while they were waiting for Ansgar to bring them the Saviour.

I particularly admired an energetic, young lecturer from Copenhagen, Harald Risbjerg, and I found excuses to talk to him whenever possible. Risbjerg was thin and narrow-shouldered. A thick moustache overbalanced his receding chin, and his hazel eyes were small and close-set behind steel-rimmed glasses. To me, he was as handsome as Mikael Gyldendal because I was susceptible to seduction by the mind.

One afternoon he lectured on the Norse view of women from earliest times, telling how the ancients treated their women with gentleness, courtesy, and respect at a time when females in other parts of the world were considered no better than animals.

Leaning forward with great intensity, he said, "They believed there was something sacred and divine in woman!"

Thrilled, I scarcely could wait for the end of the lecture, when I planned to put my divinity at Herr Risbjerg's disposal. I knew that he customarily enjoyed a cigar and a stroll down the gravel path after this session, and if I reached him first, I might be his companion. When he dismissed us, I hurried to the lectern and waited while a long line of students spoke with him. Then, as he walked away, I skipped into step beside him, afraid that he would hear the pounding of my heart.

"A fine day, Amalie," he said, holding the door for me.

He smelled of cigars and leather book bindings. His nearness struck me dumb, but I knew I must say something or he would get away from me. Rigmor Hansen was lurking behind us, waiting to snatch him.

"What is a woman's place in life, Herr Risbjerg?"

He smiled quizzically. "That depends on the woman."

"What you said today makes me think I could do anything"—I flung my arms wide—"be anything!"

"Ah, you Northern women," he laughed. "I have not married because I do not think I could manage one of you!"

"But why must we be managed? We are as good as men!"

"If we must discuss the Woman Question on such a beautiful day, let me approach it this way. Have you heard the story of the shepherdess who fell in love with a chimneysweep?" He scratched his moustache with one finger. An unlovely gesture, I thought, hating myself for noticing anything that made him less than perfect.

He lit his cigar and spoke through a rising cloud of bluish smoke. "The shepherdess followed her chimneysweep to the rooftops, enduring the difficult ascent only to say, 'I cannot bear it. This world is too large. I have followed you into the wide world; now, if you really love me, you may follow me home again.' Now, Amalie, what does this story tell you about woman's place in life?"

"She can climb—"

"But only to capture her chimneysweep. The story doesn't tell us the sweep's answer to her challenge, but we both can guess that he did follow her home. She bound him to the earth."

"*I* would stay on the rooftops," I said stubbornly.

"So they all say, but it ends differently!" He laughed. "And that is why I stay away from shepherdesses! Go find your lambs, Amalie; I must meet with Andreas Korfits."

His dismissal enraged me. Feeling hurt and demeaned, I went back to the dormitory to read Leonora Christina's *Memories of Woe*. Because of a man, her husband, Leonora Christina spent twenty-one years locked up in the Blue Tower in Copenhagen. Men!

Kristine Langelund, my best friend at Sandinge, rescued me from my gloom with some of her tall tales. Kristine's favorites were the stories of Mols, where the people love to make fun of themselves.

"The people of Mols decided to save their church bell from the enemy, so they rowed it out to sea in a boat and dropped it over the side. Then, to be sure they could find it again, they marked the side of the boat!" Kristine laughed heartily, slapping her thighs with both hands.

I laughed too, but not hard enough to suit her, so she tried another story.

"Did you hear about the group in Mols that wanted to know how many tickets to buy for a concert?"

I had rather enjoyed composing my personal *Memories of Woe* and wasn't sure I wanted to be cheered, but neither did I want to offend Kristine. I asked her to tell me about them.

"They kept counting themselves and losing track until a stranger came along and suggested that they stick their noses in the mud and count the holes. They did this and were well pleased with the results."

We both laughed until the tears came, though part of my mind told me the story wasn't funny. I knew I never would get it straight if I tried to tell it, and people would look at me strangely. I asked Kristine why I had this trouble.

"You are too serious to tell jokes," she said.

"Well, I know one, but it isn't really a joke, It's true. A fisherman was to be married, and when the pastor asked if he would have the girl as his wife, he turned around to the others in the church and asked, 'Say, good friends, will any of you have her?' When they all answered 'No' he said, 'Then neither will I!' and there was no wedding. That really happened in Hals. Hop-Caroline swears it!"

Kristine's face grew serious, and with the tears of laughter still wet on her cheeks, she looked most doleful. "Poor girl! If it really happened, it's hard to laugh at."

"Awful things that happen seem funny a long time after, don't you think?"

"Think?" Kristine puffed out her cheeks with mock pomposity. "So, Sandinge! Great thoughts have come from there! Come, Amalie, we are to have raspberry *rødgrød* for *middag*."

I hadn't realized the raspberries were ripe enough for red porridge, but Kristine knew the time of everything that grew, almost to the day. She was of real peasant stock, coming from a family that had worked for the same landowners for generations.

When the Folk High Schools first opened, the privileged classes objected to giving ordinary people too much education, fearing they would become "too good to dig ditches and spread manure," but when these misgivings proved to be unfounded, the gentry went in for peasant glorification, which Kristine found amusing.

"They wear smocks and sabots and send their daughters to milk the cows," she said. "They look too silly, and the poor cows! Think how they must feel—being tugged at by weak, little hands that cannot unburden them!"

Although my hands had not milked cows, they were strong enough, and I proved it by gripping Kristine's fingers tightly and repeating Bishop Grundtvig's motto, "Stick to the earth, it will serve us best!"

Giggling in our delight at being friends beyond class, we ran to the dining hall, where I reaffirmed my belief in Kristine's oracular powers. Big tureens of jewel-red porridge stood on all the tables.

Though I forgot it briefly, I returned to the memory of my humiliating talk with Herr Risbjerg again and again. It drove me to search for examples of women who had climbed to the rooftops and stayed there, with or without their chimney-sweeps.

I found much to admire in Margrethe, Denmark's un-crowned queen. She was intelligent, shrewd, and never violent. Married to King Haakon of Norway, she was wid-owed very young and ruled through her son Olaf. She never married again, undoubtedly by her own choice, because even the most rough and primitive of the Scandinavian nobles ad-mired her and submitted to her will. Though we were told that the alabaster effigy on Margrethe's tomb at Roskilde was idealized, I was certain that she had been beautiful. The idea of her was beautiful.

When Kristine told me about the Girl Market where the farmers came to hire help, describing how the men went about feeling the muscles in arms bared to the shoulder, I pondered the chasm between girls for hire and Margrethe, the Semiramis of the North. I pictured myself somewhere near the middle of a swinging bridge between the two, and I resolved to inch my way toward the Dame of Our Kingdoms.

However, I found myself skipping to the other side of the bridge very soon.

One early September morning not long after I came home from Sandinge I offered to hang up the sheets behind the trees of the lower garden. This was Hop-Caroline's job, but I had noticed that she was getting older, and the heavy weight of a basket of wet linens nearly overbalanced her. It was to be a warm, green and gold day, but the grass gleamed with dew, and I walked barefoot to the lines with my steaming, lye-scented load. As I approached, two black and white magpies took to the air noisily. Their clamor alerted the white doves that gave our home its name, bringing them from their cotes in a burst like an out-of-season snowstorm. I stood still for a moment to watch them descend on the grain Sven Rasmussen had scattered for them, then tucked up my skirt, knotted a kerchief over my hair, and rolled my sleeves.

As I flung the hot, wet sheets over the line, I heard wheels rolling along the road from Ausig, but I didn't look around until a man's voice called out, "*God dag!* Can you tell me the whereabouts of Herr Shipowner Ormstrup?"

I whirled, snatching the kerchief from my hair and pulling the hem of my skirt from my waistband. I supposed the stranger had appraised a completely immodest stretch of bare leg at some length before he spoke.

He was the best-looking man I ever had seen as he sat there in a shiny, red-trimmed trap behind a glossy black horse. His chestnut hair and goatee glinted in the sun, which threw a shadow of his strong nose and chin on the sheet I had just smoothed. His full lips stretched in a smile.

"Don't be bashful, charming as it is. I need information, my girl!"

Your girl indeed, I thought. *What do you take me for?*

He cocked his head to consider me. "You were such a picture before I surprised you! The best of the land, noble in the simplicity of your dignified labor—but now you've become self-conscious. Too bad!"

I knew then what I had to deal with. Here was a peasant-worshiper of the deepest dye. Normally I would have laughed at such pretensions, but those hazel eyes almost the color of dark amber held too many complications for quick dismissal. I remembered Jette's words, "We must seem to be what men imagine. They invent the women they love." This man who still waited for me to speak had invented a peasant girl, and that was what I would be, for there was a sudden heat between us. I felt it, and he must have, for the reins slipped from his hands as we stared at each other.

I finally found my voice and told him, "Herr Shipowner Ormstrup is taking his coffee in the garden."

"I will ask your master if I may take you for a drive when my business with him is finished."

"No!" I said. "He would not allow it. When you have finished your business, I will meet you at the edge of the heath—just over there." I pointed to a spot not visible from the windows of Dovedale and turned back to my work as he drove on.

When I had stretched the remaining sheets haphazardly on the line, I hurried to the spot. I pinched my cheeks furiously, then decided it was too soon. The color would fade before he came. I pulled off some purple broom to thrust into my hair, but the steam had straightened the curls left over from the Sabbath, and the flowers slipped out as quickly as I put them in.

Why didn't he hurry? But if he did, what would I say? I didn't know his name, and he didn't know mine. The whole thing was insane! I got up from the heather to run away, only to come back and throw myself down to wait.

When he did come, he left the trap in the road and walked to me. He had a handsome stride that bit off distance as if he owned the heath. His pockets were full of Mor's almond cookies, and he was delighted with himself for managing an unexpected treat for me.

Assuming there was nothing about me to be told, that I was the personification of all the general peasant virtues—and vices, I suppose—he told me about himself. He was Peter Jorgen from the island of Funen, where his parents lived in a manor house his twin brothers would inherit. The law of primogeniture being no respecter of station, he had gone to business rather than to the Church, and he had come to Ausig to discuss an important arrangement with Herr Shipowner Ormstrup.

"He is a good businessman," he said. "I think we will have a long and fruitful association—unless he finds out that I mean to steal you! One cannot find good workers as in the old days."

"Have you tried the Girl Market?"

"Let *him* go there, for I will have you!" He leaned close to me. "And not for work!"

"But I know how to do everything!"

"I'm sure you do," he said, and kissed me until I was as weak as when I fell in the snow on my way to Holger Danske. I struggled, knowing I could not claim his kiss until he knew who I was.

"I will be missed if I don't go back!"

"We can meet tonight. I have been invited to return for *middag.*"

"Things may be different tonight," I warned.

He bowed, as he had been taught, no doubt in the manor house on Funen. "I must have something of yours to touch until we meet again."

I pulled the amber cross from my neck and dropped it into his palm, leaving him to puzzle over its fine quality.

That night I was late coming to the table, and Mor sent Hop-Caroline upstairs for me. I had been crying and sighing all afternoon, afraid to face Peter Jorgen after my deception.

I had, however, put on my newest dress of deep blue silk and was ready except for my hair, which Hop-Caroline unceremoniously raked with a brush. At the door I broke from her clutch and unstoppered Jette's perfume to scent the base of my throat.

"So you've heard what a fine young cock we have at table tonight!" she chortled.

I moaned.

Peter Jorgen rose when I entered the room, completely concealing the confusion he must have felt. He followed Mor's conversational lead for a while, then branched out on his own topics, chiefly the refusal of the University of Copenhagen to install Georg Brandes in the Chair of Belles Lettres because he had said that Jesus Christ would diminish in importance as Thor and Odin had.

"A terrible thing!" Mor said.

"Indeed it is!" Peter said. "No professor should be measured by his orthodoxy."

Mor tightened her lips, for she had meant that Brandes' views were terrible, and Peter quickly changed the subject to performances he had lately seen at the Royal Theatre: a Holberg comedy and the dancing of *Coppelia*.

When Far suggested that I show the garden to our guest, Peter pulled back my chair with great courtliness and draped my shawl around my shoulders.

As we walked in the cool night without a word, I lost the poise of the dinner table completely. I was terrified of the coming showdown. All at once Peter started to laugh. It was a great, booming, unfettered sound—the laughter of Funen, whose people are called the Bavarians of Denmark.

Relieved and angry at the same time, I said, "I'm glad that we have afforded you some amusement during your visit."

"Frøken Nielsen, you are all women rolled into one! What

an exquisite joke!"

"Then you aren't angry?"

"Angry? I'm delighted! I can't afford a mistress, and my parents are scarcely emancipated enough to accept a peasant daughter-in-law, so your true identity solves my problem. Will you have me?"

"But we are strangers to each other!"

"Stop making foolish objections. We both know what we know, is that not true? We have known since this morning."

"Say my name."

"Amalie!" He made it sound rich and queenly, as I thought it should, and I went to him gladly.

This was my own fairy tale, I thought, until he released me and gave me a slap on the rear that stung right through my petticoats. Throwing his head back with that lusty Funen laugh, he said, "Our children will outnumber the bastards of Christian IV!"

8

Peter and I were to be married on June 5, Danish Constitution Day. He argued that it should be much sooner, but I had been reading when I might have been sewing on the obligatory dozen of everything that a bride must bring to her marriage, and besides, Far wanted us to know each other better.

Gradual discovery was impossible for us because Peter traveled in his business, but when he came to Dovedale, our betrothal allowed us to be alone together, and we took full advantage of the privilege up to a point. I was unwilling to go the way of Hanne Eskildsen, who had borne a husky baby boy six months after her wedding day.

Between Peter's widely spaced visits, I embroidered linens until my eyes watered, hoping to finish everything but the monograms, which could not be stitched until after the ceremony. I sewed secretly in my room on the Sabbath, risking the penalty of taking those stitches up with my nose in heaven. Heaven could wait, but Peter couldn't!

We were apart at Christmas, when every Dane goes home if

he has to crawl. Thinking of Peter on Funen, I stood apart from the celebration of Dovedale, wasting what would be my last Yule at Ausig.

A candle shone from every window and a sheaf of rye for the birds was nailed to the hitching post in the courtyard. Hop-Caroline, now completely gray, hobbled to the attic with a dish of porridge for *nissen,* the Christmas elf, and the red-berried Christ's-thorn crowned every doorway.

Dovedale was filled with neighbors and friends all the twelve days of Christmas. If anyone should go out of the house without partaking of its cheer, they would bear our Yule away, and though no one refused our sweets and ale, Mor took the extra precaution of filling the pockets of departing guests with peppernuts.

On Christmas Eve, the lucky almond in the pudding fell to me. I think Hop-Caroline nudged the treasure my way, but all to no avail, for luck cannot be manipulated.

In early January, I developed a fever that baffled the doctor in Ausig. Tossing in delirium, I asked for what I dared not request when I was in full possession of myself; the presence of my real mother and my brother Ib at the wedding. Far promised to send for them, thinking I would not live to hold him to his word. I had no intention of dying, and my greatest suffering was the dread of having Peter see me as I was. My hair came out in great clumps, and Hop-Caroline told me I looked like a starved horse.

"Some bride you will be!" she said with cheerful malice on a dark day in February when I was inspecting myself in a hand mirror. Luckily for her, I was too weak to throw the glass.

I ordered all mirrors to be taken from my room and set about willing myself to be well. By mid-May, my hair had grown back in a soft aureole, but the emaciation was stubborn, and the fitting of my wedding gown could wait no longer. The seamstress from Ausig moved into an upstairs room to fly at the task of cutting down the ivory silk wedding dress and the seven trousseau costumes made when I was in full health.

Heartsick over my skeletal appearance, I resorted to Jette's suggestion of handkerchiefs in the bodice, then worried about cheating Peter.

He came to Dovedale two days before the wedding, and when I saw the familiar trap enter the courtyard, I turned from the window and cried. Then, hearing his voice booming in the rooms below, I lost my pride in the longing to see him.

Nothing fit me but my trousseau dresses. I put on the pale blue linen and started down the stairs clutching the railing. The upturned faces of Far, Mor, and Hop-Caroline blurred, and I saw only the hugeness of Peter as he took the stairs in a few strides to lift me and carry me down.

"Amalie, my dearest love! What has happened to you? Why wasn't I told?"

"I wouldn't allow it. I had hoped to be better by now, but the fever has made me ugly, and if you don't want me like this, you are free!"

Mor touched Far's arm and they started toward the parlor, sweeping Hop-Caroline with them to leave us alone.

"Nothing could make me stop wanting you! I have a strange fever too, Amalie, I burn for your very bones!"

"They are very close to the surface, as you see."

"I see with my heart," he said, and kissed me very gently. I had not known he could be gentle. "Funen will make you well!"

If he could love me as I was now, what could ever part us?

I asked him to carry me to the parlor, where I sat up straight on the lion head sofa and asked Far when my real mother would arrive.

"She is taking the train to Tylstrup, and Sven will meet her there tomorrow. I wonder how we will find each other after so many years?" He sighed heavily.

I saw then that Far had aged without my notice. Absorbed in my own affairs, I had failed to see the deep lines around his eyes and the sag of his once-firm cheeks. I realized too that my mother would not look as I had imagined her all my life. Far's image of her as a blooming, young woman was also mine, and I wondered if I could bear to alter it. Still, I wanted old questions answered before I started a new life with Peter.

My love was beside me, wordlessly calming my agitation with the pressure of his arm, when Sven drove into the court-yard with my mother.

Bodil Ormstrup Nielsen Pedersen was alone in the back of the carriage. She sat straight-backed with one gloved hand resting on a small suitcase. Work-worn, tired, but still proud, she was dressed all in gray, and conscious of the newness of her clothing. She barely touched the supporting hand Sven offered as she gathered her skirts to step down.

Staring at her, I saw an older version of myself. We had the same strong nose, full lips, and wide-set eyes. Her body was slightly fuller than mine had been before the fever.

"Amalie?"

With a slight pressure of his hand, Peter stepped back, and when I turned to present him, he was at the other side of the courtyard beckoning to Sven.

"*Are* you Amalie?" she asked, and I could only nod. I didn't know what to call her. Not "Mor," and certainly not

"Fru Pedersen." Nor could I call her "Bodil."

She took my hands and looked into my eyes. All strangeness melted in our tears as we embraced. For all the care Mor had given me, I never had had this fierce, unquestioning caring from her.

I saw Far's face in the window and knew that he was fighting the tears that only women were allowed. Then he was running into the courtyard to hug his sister so roughly that her bonnet fell off. Mor came from the doorway to welcome her sister-in-law to Dovedale, and with the three of us talking at once, we made slow progress to the house.

"Where is my brother Ib?"

"Gone to *Amerika*. He is a Mormon now—"

"And Tinus Pedersen?" Far asked.

"Dead these six months. Tuberculosis, they said. Now Karsten, what have you done to this girl? I gave you a fat, rosy baby, and look at her now! Ah, Maren, how long it has been—"

I turned from the happy tangle of reunion to see Peter watching us with his hands in his pockets an outsider. I would not have it so. As I presented him to my mother, my legs weakened under me, and he took me to the garden to rest on the bench under the shade of the beeches.

"A new mother and a new husband at the same time is too much for anyone," he said.

"What do you think of my mother?"

"She is a good woman."

"Is that all you can say about her?"

"What you cannot say briefly, you do not know."

Because of my physical weakness, tears came with little provocation, and I found slights where none were intended. If Peter found my mother so unremarkable, how would be look upon me as I aged? As I pulled away from him in my unreasonable hurt, a shocking oversight of my own occurred to me.

"Peter! What about *your* parents? When are they coming?"

"They are here—at the inn in Ausig. When I told my mother of your illness, she refused to lay the burden of meeting upon you before the wedding. She says you can come to know each other at Fairwoods."

"But I would think she would want to look me over—decide whether I will do as a wife for you!"

Peter laughed. "She knows that the matter is beyond her say!" Then he kissed me with a controlled intensity that charged the very air around us.

I went to bed in the middle of the afternoon to store up strength for the next day, but I didn't sleep. Peter came and went in the room, Far and Mor were in and out with a hovering concern, and Hop-Caroline sat at the foot of my bed to chatter about the preparations whenever she could escape her part in them.

"They have put up the two masts with the welcome banner and the garland of fir is on the door—the flags must wait until tomorrow, in case it rains in the night—Herr Ormstrup has gone to the attic for the painted shields—oh, it will be so fine!" She clapped her hands like a young girl.

Seeing the fold of a gray skirt at the edge of the door, I called, "Please come in!"

My real mother entered the room with quiet diffidence and sat in the chair Hop-Caroline pulled close to the bed.

"Two mothers you have," Hop-Caroline observed as she hobbled away; "you will have all the advice that any bride could wish!"

"What advice do I need?" I asked when we were alone.

"Much cannot be told," she said in a slow, measured way that showed she had given the matter considerable thought.

"Your Peter can provide for you?"

"Oh yes, he is very clever in business."

"That's good, for when the stall is empty, the horses bite each other."

"Has the stall been empty for you?"

"Sometimes, Amalie, not always. Karsten has helped many times. Your husband will be away from you much of the time?"

"I suppose so. He travels as far as Hamburg and Paris."

She sighed. "It has always been for women to wait. They might as well learn it first as last. Well, you do love him, I can see that. I saw you with him in the garden, and there was a glow around the two of you like the ring around the moon when the weather is about to change. It was like that with me and Niels Ibsen."

Since she had opened the door to the question that troubled me most, I seized the chance to ask it.

"I—I have been sick. How much strength does it take to—to be a wife to a man?"

She laughed. "If your Peter had been the one with the fever, you might worry, for they say, 'When the Devil is ill, a monk he would be, but when he is well, then a devil is he!' But a woman can give herself no matter how she feels—can if she will. At first, take your pleasure in his, and when you are well, your own joy will catch up with you!"

I caught her hand and kissed the work-roughened palm, feeling closer to her than I ever had to Mor. "Oh, why didn't you keep me?"

She averted her face. "As Karsten has told you, I hope, I loved you and wanted you to have a better life."

"But which would have been better?" I cried.

"What's done is done."

In the morning, I felt uncommonly well. I hummed to myself as Mor, my mother, and Hop-Caroline helped me dress and assured me that the many tucks in the ivory silk concealed my wasted condition.

The guests would arrive for *snaps* and ale at ten, and I would sit behind closed doors in the parlor, unseen until I was seated in the carriage for the ride to the church. Hurrying through the rose-filled rooms, I reached my hiding place as the first carriage stopped in the courtyard.

My future in-laws alighted from the rented barouche. Herr Jorgen was a portly man who walked with a cane, and I diagnosed a case of gout from his heavily veined red nose. Clearly he was an active man who bore his hindering affliction with impatience. As he stood in the sunny courtyard taking in Dovedale with a sweeping glance, I saw much of Peter in him.

Fru Jorgen was tall and slender in a watered-silk gown the color of a thrush's wing. She had a porcelain refinement of feature seldom seen in our region of North Jutland, and the hand she placed on Sven's arm as she stepped down was as white as the meat of an almond. She was a queen, I thought, staring at her in awed admiration. She seemed to float between the greenery-twined masts that held the welcome banner, and I felt a twinge of black jealousy. Her presence would take all eyes from the bride.

But later, when the guests crowded around the flower-decked carriage to admire me, she stood back, smiling at me from a distance as she let me have my day. When the laughing, jostling neighbors hurried to their own carriages to begin the ride to the church, she moved close enough to say, "Lucky the bride the sun shines on!"

At the church, Peter lifted me down, and Pastor Madsen walked through the open doors to meet us and lead us inside, where candles flickered in the swimming green light.

The strength I had felt earlier was ebbing away, and the bridal wreath of myrtle weighed heavily on my head. I drew on the vitality of Peter standing so straight beside me, raising my chin to lock it in an imaginary vise. I'm sure that Pastor Madsen shortened his sermon to save my meager strength, for I remember little more than the solemn vows we took.

Then we were in the sun again, smiling from the flowery carriage at the head of the procession. Whips cracked and guns went off; horses reared and women screamed. The noise was joyful, but it made me tremble, and Peter put a protective arm around me.

At Dovedale, a band of musicians from Brønderslev struck up a new tune every time a carriage set down a load of wedding guests. House and garden were aswarm with visitors eating, drinking, and talking gaily.

Peter took me straight to my room and put me to bed, insisting that I sleep while he sat beside me holding my hand.

"Lock the door," I said, and when he had, I threw back the cover and held out my arms to him. What a picture I must have made with those thin arms poking out of a welter of bridal petticoats!

He began a solicitous protest, then broke off with a burst of laughter and came to me. In that narrow, girlish bed with a myrtle blossom wreath hanging rakishly on its headpost, we both forgot that I was a near invalid. Warned by my mother not to expect pleasure at first, I gave myself to the encounter with a fierce interest. So this was what a man was like! The hardness, the hairiness, the power, all of it mine! I took it greedily, even the pain, as we met each other and fell back like the waters of Skagen.

Later, when we came downstairs for the food, speeches, and

dancing, Far remarked on my improved color and said the rest must have done me good. I smiled and walked with my arm in Peter's to the center table, where a flowerbed of blossoms surrounded a huge, flat cake decorated with our initials in raspberry jam. Understanding the jokes and glances of our friends better than they knew, I cut the first piece of cake and stood back to gaze at the tall candles burning at each end of the table. They represented Peter and me, and if both flamed until midnight, we would have a long life together. The wax was of the best quality, and the wicks were strong.

Just before midnight, I saw that one of the candles was missing from its holder. It worried me, but when I mentioned it to Peter, he said, "Never mind, some prankish boy has run away with it. Come, the carriage is ready!"

Driving under an arch of flowers and then between a double row of torches along the lane, I looked back at my family in the lighted door of Dovedale. I couldn't see their faces, but their arms were uplifted in farewell, and I could hear them shouting, "God bless!"

PART TWO

Two Tapers Burning

88

9

Peter had wanted to sail the Kattegat to Funen, but by the time our ship reached the Mariager fjord, I had had more than enough of the water and begged to finish the journey overland to Fredericia, where we would cross the Little Belt to his island home.

"I will never sail again!" I swore as we climbed into the coach leaving Hadsund.

"You don't know what real sailing is," said Peter laughing. "We hugged the shore all the way, and the Kattegat is calm when Jutland stops the wind from the west."

I soon found the jarring of the coach as distressing as the tilting and rolling of the ship, but I said nothing and tried to appreciate the scenery that Peter found so entrancing.

"Look! Isn't that a perfect Watteau canvas? Misty, soft— with the little hills melting into a modulated horizon—"

When Peter was in Paris, he often went to the Louvre to admire the paintings, saying that the French captured the look of Denmark so much better than our own artists. I asked if many Frenchmen came to Denmark to paint, and he said they did not. They painted other scenes in a way that evoked Denmark in a morning mist or in the late afternoon when the shadows were soft.

Peter knew so many things that I did not. We spent one whole day of the journey in the roles of language teacher and pupil, and at the end of it, the few phrases of faltering French that I could repeat seemed hardly worth the effort. My response to Peter was anything but cerebral.

"Never mind," he said indulgently. "*Je t'adore!*"

Peter's travels had spurred his interest in the differences and similarities between our own people and those of other lands. He found many of the differences attractive.

"Take the Irish, Amalie. They catch our imagination! Something disciplined in the Dane hails the undisciplined in the Irish. They complement us with something we lack."

Remembering Far's long-ago words at Skagen, I said, "Could it be sublimity?"

"Clever girl, that may be it!"

Peter's praise warmed me like a tile stove, but I worried about stretching my mind to meet his—until we stopped at an inn for the night. Then, happiness in the bed of love was all that mattered, and I forgot that Peter's thoughts ran so far ahead of mine that I could not hope to catch up.

My incomplete recovery from the fever and the tension of trying to meet Peter's every expectation combined to blur my first impression of Fairwoods. I was very ill when we reached Fredericia. The doctor Peter summoned wanted to keep me there for several weeks, but I begged to go on.

The huge carriage from the manor met us at Faarup. Its wheels were as high as my head, and the driver who helped Peter lift me to the cushioned seat wore green and gold livery.

When Peter told me that Fairwoods would be visible

beyond the beech grove just ahead, I actually held my eyes open with my fingers to see it, but all I had was a quick glimpse of its rosy brick hugeness at the end of a lime tree avenue before I passed from consciousness.

I awoke deep in a silk-covered featherbed and stared upward at sculptured plaster *amorini* cavorting on the ceiling. Pale rose draperies were drawn at the tall windows, creating a pink twilight in the room, and long-stemmed pink roses arranged in a stiff fan on the marble mantel scented the air. What was I doing in this strange, perfect room, and where was Peter? I must get up and find him.

I tried to throw the *dyne* from me, but it was so heavy and so slippery in its silk that I fell back against the double pillows, exhausted by the effort. Then the door opened cautiously.

"Peter?" I called.

"You're awake, ma'am?" A plump little female in a black-and-white costume that made her look like a magpie scudded noiselessly to the bedside to look me over with a deferential curiosity. Everything about her was round; her eyes, her cheeks, the end of her turned-up nose, and her body, which was pulled in at the waist like a sausage by her tight apron strings.

"Who are you?"

"I am Frida, ma'am, I am to look after you."

"Well, Frida, I hope I will be well soon so you won't have to look after me."

"Oh, ma'am, I am to do for you, sick or well, as long as you are at Fairwoods. Fru Jorgen has said it!"

"A fine thing for me to arrive like a sack of malt! Did Peter carry me in?"

"The men carried you on a litter. Herr Jorgen had allowed everyone to come up from the fields and the dairy to greet

Master Peter's bride. It was to be a holiday like the times when Master Dines and Master Dich brought their new wives to Fairwoods."

"And I spoiled it!"

"Oh no! You gave them a few hours off this time, and Herr Jorgen has promised another celebration later when you are well. You have done better for them than Jonna or Mathilde!"

"The wives of Peter's brothers?"

Frida nodded with a barely concealed grimace, then added quickly, "I should not call them Jonna and Mathilde. I forgot myself. They will be the mistresses of Fairwoods someday." The prospect did not seem to please her.

"Where is my husband?"

"Just back from riding with his brothers. I will tell him you are awake. Shall I bring chocolate or coffee? Master Peter takes coffee at this hour."

"Then I will have it too," I said, wondering what the hour was. I had begun a new life while I was out of my body and was confused by returning to myself in this Marie Antoinette room complete with a personal maid. Peter was my only link with remembered reality.

He strode into the room with the smell of horses strong on him, marking the pale blue rug with his boots as he came. Frida followed him like a small, adoring shadow to set a tray beside the bed and pour out coffee into two Royal Copenhagen cups. She left quickly when Peter bent to kiss me.

"You look a thousand times better! The doctor must have been right to bar me from this room until you could rest."

Soothed to know that he had not been absent by choice, I asked, "How was your ride?"

"Those brothers of mine can best me at horsemanship, and

I sweat like a peasant before they think to take off their gloves! Dines, that fox, took me out to see the single tree he planted in a field to make it forest land subject to lower taxes. Now! Are you strong enough to meet the family?"

I started to push up from the pillows once more, but he thrust my shoulders back very gently. "You don't have to get up. Frida will help you with your hair, and they will come to you."

"To my bed?" I was shocked.

Peter laughed. "You will hold a levee. Frida!" As she hurried in, he opened the door of the tall, creamy wardrobe, and I was startled to see it filled with my own dresses. "Where do you keep those lacy little things that women wear in bed?"

I started to speak, but Frida said it for me. "She has none, Master Peter."

I was ashamed of my lack, but Peter chuckled. "Damned if I'd noticed! Go steal one of Jonna's, Frida, and if she complains, tell her I'll buy her a new one."

I always blamed this pre-emption of Jonna's lacy bed shawl for her immediate and lasting dislike of me, but there were other factors that I wouldn't examine—like her being in love with Peter. Jonna was Dich's wife. She was a cold-looking silver blonde from Korsor, and though she seemed devoid of emotion, she seethed with it. She looked down on me and mocked my Jutland accent.

When I asked Peter if he found her attractive, he said, "As a piece of porcelain, she does very well," which answered my question and raised others I knew I never would ask.

Mathilde, Dines' wife, was placid and lazy. She had produced a baby in each of the three years she had been married to the dark twin, putting them in the care of the servants while she gorged on sweets and awaited the next arrival. Her father owned a shipyard at Odense, and she had been reared in luxury. She reminded me of a blooded mare that never got any exercise. Mathilde was not unkind, she simply took no interest in me.

As for Peter's twin brothers, I preferred Dich. He was the fairer of the two and displayed less of the arrogant cunning I found so disturbing in Dines. Also, I may have felt sorry for him because he was married to a woman like Jonna.

One evening when I was well enough to walk in the garden, I decided to stroll toward the stables. Herr Jorgen kept a liver-colored gelding named Viggo that reminded me of Brand, and when I felt homesick for Dovedale, I would stroke his soft nose for comfort. Approaching Viggo's stall, I heard the voices of Dines and Dich in the tack room.

"He was a damned fool to marry her!" Dines said.

My face grew hot, for I was certain they were talking about me.

"Nobody is a damned fool to marry the woman he loves," Dich said, adding sadly, "if she loves *him*. She does, you know."

Yes, I did, and I blessed Dich for knowing it.

Peter was away much of the time, and without him I found it hard to fit into the life at Fairwoods. On Sunday afternoons the coachman drove us to the neighboring manor houses to visit, and I felt like a spinster aunt whose presence was dutifully tolerated.

Other days I read, sewed, or walked in the gardens with their big stone vases and clipped privet hedges. A tiny stream wound through the flower beds, and swans floated on its slow-moving surface with their untidy-looking cygnets.

Fru Jorgen spoke to me at mealtimes and when we passed in the wide, parquet-floored halls, but her detached manner left me lonely. I respected her because she was Peter's mother, but I could not love her.

Herr Jorgen, when he noticed me at all, stared hard at my stomach to see if it was swelling with a child. He was very interested in such matters, and Frida, who was my only real friend at Fairwoods, told me that well he might be. Many of the children who played around the kitchen had been sired by him.

What Jonna and Mathilde did with their days was beyond my knowledge. After a huge breakfast in the dining room, they would disappear into their own wings of the house, not to be seen again until *middag*.

The lack of anything useful to do drove me to the kitchen one morning, and I plunged into the jamming operation there with the greatest of pleasure until a scandalized Frida hauled me away from the steaming kettles of fruit.

"You mustn't, ma'am, it isn't fitting!"

I fought tears, thinking that if Peter didn't come back soon, I would run away—go back to Dovedale, where I could do anything I pleased.

Some things were expected of me, however. When guests were coming for dinner, I would be informed of their interests early in the day so that I might gather information for adequate conversation. Instructions as to my dress were given to Frida, and she worked over my costume and coiffure for hours.

Feeling miscast in my role, I came downstairs at the signal from Fru Jorgen. The main stairs were broad enough to accommodate the wide skirts of the three Jorgen daughters-in-law walking abreast. Jonna always took the middle position, knowing that the light from the chandelier at the foot of the stairs struck her white shoulders to best advantage when she was in the center. Mathilde was busy repairing some flaw in her attire that had passed unnoticed until Jonna mentioned it in a sharp, brittle aside. When we reached the foyer, Dich and Dines claimed their wives, and I fell in behind them alone, to be claimed later by some elderly squire who would offer me sherry and the creaking gallantry of good breeding.

The broad hall to the drawing room was set with slender panels of mirror between the dark paintings of classical scenes. Passing the mirrors, we created our own fleeting portraits. Fru Jorgen was a cool sapphire in a high-throated dress of lapis-lazuli, Jonna was a hard-cut diamond in dazzling white, Mathilde was a milky opal in rosy ivory, and I was a resentful emerald in a green dress that had belonged to Jonna. Nothing of my own was adequate for the occasion.

I nibbled my way through seven courses, sipping at the appropriate wines and addressing alternate remarks to the guests on either side, longing for Peter. He came before the after-dinner speeches and breezily snatched me from the table.

When we were in our own rooms, we kissed hungrily, and Jonna's green dress soon lay in a ring beside the bed.

Then Peter said, "I have a surprise for you! I wasn't going to speak until I could show it to you, but I can't wait! I was gone so long this time because I was arranging to be with you always. Traveling is fine when you take your heart with you, miserable when you leave it behind! How would you like to be an innkeeper's wife?"

"That would depend on the innkeeper!" I said.

"I am the innkeeper! I have brought a hostel in Odense."

"Oh Peter, you'll be home all day—every day!"

"We will be together every day and working very hard to make Gammel Hjem the best inn on Funen!"

10

We took over Gammel Hjem in October. The Old Home. I liked the name. It was comfortable and welcoming. When Peter drove me to Odense to see it for the first time, we passed Egeskov Castle with its round, turreted towers and step gables rising pink from the water that doubled them. The castle's dream-like beauty convinced me that I was living in a fairy tale. My health restored, I was escaping the oppressive spell of Fairwoods to live happily ever after with Peter.

The Jorgens were not pleased with Peter's venture, and since he had spent his entire inheritance for the inn, he could expect no more help from them. Neither could we expect them to visit us in such a common establishment. We were free!

Peter was so proud of his prize that I tried not to notice the broken roof tiles. The small-paned casement windows were smeary with smoke and grease, and when we went inside, I gasped at the sight of a rush-strewn floor.

"Who owned this place, Prince Amleth?" I asked, kicking at the fusty rushes glued together with spilled food and drink. I tucked my skirt into my waistband and looked around for a bucket. "What we need is a pitchfork!"

"Amalie, don't—I'll hire someone—at least until some vagrant is thrown into the jail."

"What jail?"

"It's part of the inn. Didn't you see the bars as we came in? We feed the prisoners, and they work for us in return."

"Why didn't you tell me this before?"

"I didn't think it was important"—he smiled anxiously— "but it's a good arrangement—"

"Oh, a fine arrangement! I've always longed to be murdered in my bed!"

"They are not murderers, Amalie, just debtors, loiterers, and petty offenders. You needn't be afraid. Do you think I would endanger you?" His eyes flashed and he folded his arms across his chest, turning slightly away from me.

I ran my finger inside the rim of a tankard which had been left unwashed. The dried ale was as hard as porcelain glaze. Had Peter been blind when he bought this place, or was I blind not to see his vision? The shrewd good sense of Jutland told me that he had made a mistake, but I would not say so.

"Well, since we have no prisoners to do it, let's clean this place ourselves. Even a pig would scorn it now!"

We worked far into the night, piling the filthy rushes behind the inn, scrubbing the rough planks underneath, and wiping down cobwebs from the beams. Peter was energetic but clumsy, and as long as he considered it a game, he worked happily, but I was fiercely serious from the first, determined to make Gammel Hjem look as he had described it to me.

When we were too exhausted to go on, we staggered into the cool night to look at the mysterious curtains and searchlights of fire called the aurora borealis.

"I will never let you work this hard again," Peter whispered, holding me inside his coat, "but you were magnificent—like one of the warrior maidens of the old times!"

The moment ended with the emptying of a chamber pot from a nearby window. As the ammonia odor drifted our way, we laughed and went inside to sleep in our coats, too weary to look for bedding that surely would be too filthy to use. We did not make love, but it was a tender night.

We were alone in Gammel Hjem for several weeks while we were making it ready for guests, and this was our happiest time there.

The inn stood at the eastern edge of Odense, facing west. When I polished the many-paned windows, they caught the setting sun, offering it as a blazing invitation to travelers, and we had to turn a few away because we were not yet ready. This made us work all the harder.

Great barrels of madeira and brandy were wheeled into the bar, new copper tankards shone from the shelves, and the heavy, oak table and bench were scrubbed until they looked like freshly cut wood. I polished the three-legged corner chairs with carved backs until they gleamed.

Peter experimented happily with the old Funen wall decorations, cutting patterns in potatoes and dipping them in red and blue dye to stencil designs on the walls of the festival room. He bought hand-woven cloth in blue and white and was delighted with the curtains I made from it. We replenished the blue-and-white crockery in the corner cupboard and stacked new linens in the huge chest covered with floral painting.

The bars on the windows of the guest rooms troubled me, and I said, "People will think the whole inn is a jail! Can't we take those things out?"

"You will be glad for them!" said Peter. "I have taken

some pains to learn the rules of innkeeping, and one of the first is this: when a fight breaks out, lock the doors and windows. This will keep reinforcements out and bring the battle to a close more quickly. Also, certain low types have been known to climb out the window to avoid paying for their lodging."

"Surely we won't have such people here!"

"Were you expecting Copenhagen society?" He chuckled, then hugged me as he saw that I was taking the gibe poorly. "Don't worry, I'll protect you!"

In the small living room and two bedrooms we kept for our own use, we whitewashed the walls and painted everything paintable in red, appying curly, blue *J's* with the potato stencil. The rest of the inn consisted of a room for making *smørrebrød,* a washing-up room, the kitchen, a pantry, cellar, brew house, barn, and stalls for the travelers' horses. Our own matched grays were stabled on the other side of the jail and adjoining woodshed.

When everything was ready, we decided to celebrate with a fall picnic before becoming responsible business people. I packed a basket of *smørrebrød,* almond *kager,* and ale from our new stocks, and we walked a mile to the beech forest east of the inn. The leaves had passed from green to gold while we were working so hard at Gammel Hjem. Now they were shading to the soft brown of very old paper, crumbling to dust inside our shoes as we walked. A red mouse ran into the path before us and froze, fixing us with a bright, black-eyed stare.

I touched Peter's arm lightly and the mouse streaked out of sight, making a sound like thin pages turning among the leaves.

"I thought he was going to speak," I breathed. "There is something about this wood—I think it is enchanted!"

"It is when you walk in it," Peter said, and he kissed me—not at all like a husband of nearly half a year.

The sun disappeared suddenly, and a blast of wind brought a stinging downpour of rain. As we ran to escape it, I saw it turn to heavy, wet snow on my cape, but before we reached the edge of the trees, it stopped and the sun came back. We retraced the path to a fallen log and sat down to eat our food.

That is, Peter did. I couldn't. The running had upset my stomach, I thought, turning away from the sight of him enjoying the tiny sandwiches I had made from boiled eggs, spicy pressed meat, and thick, white cheese.

"We have snatched a day from winter," Peter said happily, putting the ale bottle to his lips.

We went home to light fires in the bar, the festival room, and our own small sitting room, then settled ourselves to await the uncertain arrival of our first paying guests.

The first to come, however, was a police officer with a prisoner. The unfortunate man's name was Søren Gade, we were told, and he was a habitual drunkard. This was evident from the way his watery eyes lingered on the liquor barrels. His lips were cracked, and he winced as he ran his tongue over them.

While Peter and the officer were taking him to the jail, I went to the kitchen to fix him some food. The tan, raw sausage; the egg yolks undulating in the whites; even the pale yellow butter sickened me, and I worked with my head turned aside, clutching the edge of the table to put down waves of nausea.

Throwing a napkin over the tray, I hurried to the jail. Peter had taken the police officer back to the bar. I could see them talking together as I passed. They had left the key in the lock of the cell. Letting myself in awkwardly, I advanced toward the huddled form of Søren Gade, wondering what was to prevent him from pushing me aside to escape.

"Herr Gade? I've brought food—"

He moaned and wrapped his arms around his head.

"You must eat—you'll feel better if you do—" God knows I didn't believe what I was saying!

He jerked his head up suddenly, fixing wild, staring eyes on a corner of the ceiling behind me. "Oh! Watch out! They're everywhere! The devils are after me—ohhh—" He threw himself down, clutching at my shoes, and the tray slipped from my hands, spilling the food all over his back. The sight of it on the filthy, stiff cloth of his coat was too much for me. I pulled away from him and vomited.

I forgot Søren Gade and everything but my own misery, but my sorry condition seemed to bring him out of his seizure. I felt his cracked, horny hands, strangely gentle, on my wrists, and then he was wiping my face with the napkin that had covered the tray.

"There, there, dear Fru," he soothed, "you must sit down." He pulled up the single poor chair in the cell and eased me onto it. "My good wife Asta, God rest her, always had this trouble when she was with child—"

I stared at him, not knowing whether to laugh or cry. Why hadn't I known?

"I—I'll fix you something else—I'm all right now." I hurried out, almost forgetting to turn the key in my confusion.

Ashamed of my ignorance, I tried to make excuses for it. Knowing about the gestation of farm animals was no help, for cattle and pigs didn't get sick like this. Mor had never discussed pregnancy with me, certainly, and there had been so little time to talk with my real mother. The mothers-to-be of Ausig had discussed their condition so obliquely that I was left with impressions of mystery rather than fact, and while I had the opportunity to observe Mathilde at Fairwoods, she was more like a mare than a woman.

Pride took the first slice of my joy, but when I had rationalized the reasons for not knowing, I was free to delight in what Peter and I had accomplished.

I told him as soon as the police officer left and grew furious when he all but said. "What took you so long?"

"I'm well ahead of Jonna!" I snapped, as if he had really said it.

Constraint lay between us for a whole day, but when he went into the town and brought back a satin-smooth rocking cradle of beechwood, I relented and threw my arms around his neck. Why should he kneel to me for doing the expected thing? I had been unreasonable.

As winter came on, fog settled on the inn like a close-fitting cap. The days were chokingly dark, and I felt that I was pushing against a wall of gloom. Winter was more bearable when one could look out over the misty reaches of the heath, I thought, longing for North Jutland.

I had too little to do, for Peter had hired three women to cook and tend the inn, and Søren Gade, whose sentence had expired, had stayed on to take charge of the stable and perform the heavy chores.

Darkness fell in the middle of the afternoon, and by *middag,* the bar and the festival room would be full of guests eating, drinking and laughing at fantastic tales in the close warmth. At first, I would join them, but Peter considered their talk too coarse for me, and soon I was spending the evenings alone in our small sitting room, falling asleep in my chair as I waited for Peter.

He seldom came to bed until the small hours of the morning, explaining that he had to entertain the guests and make them happy enough to speak well of Gammel Hjem.

Once in a while I would send for Søren Gade. We would sit before the fire and talk. Longing for akvavit, he sipped chocolate and told me of his life. He had labored in the Bladstrup brick works since boyhood and was so accustomed to working around the big oven that he could pull a smoking log from the fire bare-handed without feeling pain.

Tears came to his eyes when he spoke of his dead wife, Asta. She had been a parlormaid in the house of a city official, and her mistress gave her a garnet brooch as a parting gift when she went away with Søren.

"I pawned it for drink," he said miserably, "and when I told her, she didn't shed a tear. She just looked the other way and said 'Never mind, Søren, it only scratched the babies' faces.' What a saint she was!"

"I would have scratched *your* face!" I told him.

He measured me with his pale, blinking eyes and said, "You are a fierce one, Fru Jorgen, begging your pardon!"

Thus challenged, I stood suddenly and excused myself, marching straight into the festival room, where Peter sat with a table of traveling merchants and two cheap-looking women.

Imitating Mor's most commanding tone, I said, "Peter, I must speak with you!"

He had risen from his chair at my approach, and now he spoke with polite irony. "Ladies and gentlemen, my wife, Fru Jorgen."

Refusing to acknowledge the introduction, I sailed back to the sitting room like *Dronning Dagmar* with a fair wind at her back. Peter's tread shook the floorboards, and I began to doubt the wisdom of my protest even before I heard the sitting room door slam behind him. I waited stiff-backed, afraid to turn and look at him.

"That was a pretty exhibition!" he shouted, spinning me around.

"Yes, wasn't it! I saw that—that woman's hand on your sleeve! Just *how* happy do you make the guests while I'm locked in this room like a cloistered nun?"

He stared at me, then started to laugh. Doubling over, he fell into the chair Søren Gade had vacated, digging up the rug with his heels as he thrust his feet outward in a spasm of mirth.

"Stop it!" I screamed.

"Amalie, you're jealous!"

I was trembling now, clutching my arms close to my body to hide it. "If you want someone else, I don't want *you!*"

He caught me in his arms, but I struggled free, and he recaptured me to hold me so tightly that I whimpered.

"I always look at women, but only to remind myself that you are the queen of them all!"

"Then why do you leave me alone in here night after night? I saw more of you at Fairwoods!"

"When the inn is better known, I can spend less time with the guests. Now I must impress them and make them want to return. We must prosper for the sake of our child!"

"You could sell cod to Neptune!" I said ruefully, accepting a light kiss that flared into something more like a spark in a thatched roof in a high wind. Surely Peter would stay with me now; but no, he returned to the festival room.

I sighed, laughed at myself a little, and decided that no one ever would call Peter Jorgen "Amalie."

Later he woke me with the old saying, "Drink your beer before it gets stale, kiss your love before she goes to sleep! Why isn't it possible to do both?"

"It is . . ." I offered my lips, and though the *dyne* slipped to the floor, neither of us felt the cold.

Soon after Christmas, I had a letter from Mor. She wrote:

"Hop-Caroline swears she has seen the three-legged lambs gamboling around the church altar. Of course we do not believe in such things, but I wish she wouldn't talk like that. Karsten has not looked well this winter."

I tried to scoff at Hop-Caroline's lambs, as I did at most of her vast storehouse of superstitions. Even if she really had seen the mutilated lambs, it only meant that somebody in the parish would die, and that gave Death a wide selection.

Within a month, a death did occur. It was Hop-Caroline's. She was woven so closely into the fabric of my earliest memories that I couldn't imagine Dovedale without her, and the thought that I no longer existed in her kindly, feeble mind flooded me with sadness. This was a little death for me. She always had said that she wanted me to have her Bible when she was gone, and the day it came, I wrinkled her favorite Twenty-third Psalm with my tears. The marks are still there.

On the eve of *Store Bededag,* the Great Day of Prayer, the inn was empty. After we attended Lutheran services, Peter took me to Odense Cathedral to see Claus Berg's magnificent 16th century altar-piece. Berg had modeled his female martyrs after ladies of the Danish court, and they were exquisite. I kept returning to them while Peter inspected the somber, black-draped coffins in the small rooms off the nave.

Though I believed that I should not subject myself to morbid sights in my condition, I could not leave without seeing the coffin of King Canute. His bones had been arranged as close to the natural order as possible, but the perpetual stares of curious eyes gave them no rest. Almost nine centuries had passed since Canute had been slain by the peasants in his own church, but that ancient cruelty seemed to hang in the air.

Miracles were said to take place beside Canute's grave. The blind regained their sight, the lame walked, and the hopelessly ill became well. I marveled at such mercy from the murdered. In Canute's place, I would have been tempted to call down a curse, but that was the difference between Holy Canute and Wicked Amalie.

We came home to find a stranger on a black horse in the courtyard. He asked for me as he dismounted, then removed his hat and pulled a black-edged envelope from inside his cloak. Far was dead.

I begged to start for Ausig immediately, but Peter would not allow it. I went to bed weeping, and the church bells that tolled all through the hours of this fourth Friday after Easter mourned with me. My only consolation was the special blessedness of the soul that ascends on the Great Day of Prayer.

Our son was born the day of Far's funeral. Through sixteen hours of labor I struggled to send my spirit to Ausig, but the elemental event taking place in my body pulled it back to Odense. I wore my elbows raw trying to thrust myself up out of the pain.

I clutched Peter's hand until he winced. I needed him, but I wished he would go away and let me scream without shame. Finally the old midwife sent him out of the room, and then I had no time to scream. I pulled on the towels knotted to the bedposts, bore down, and went limp, beached by a receding tide of pain.

The thick form of the midwife blocked my view, and I did not know that I had borne a son until every trace of the dark blood had been whisked away and the child lay damp and throbbing in the curve of my nerveless arm.

"His name is Karsten," I murmured. "Tell Peter to come..."

Peter's breath was strong with brandy when he kissed me. "This is too hard, Amalie, too hard for you—"

"The hard thing is to say goodbye to the old Karsten and greet the young one in the same day. May our son be as fine as Far..."

The midwife's young helper gasped at my words, and later when I heard the maids at the inn gossiping in the kitchen, I realized they thought I had done a terrible thing in giving the name of the newly dead to an infant.

"It is begging for bad luck," said Nielsine.

Mette nodded, round-eyed and scared.

I scorned their fears, for young Karsten was a perfect baby, as beautifully formed as the sculptured *amorini* on the ceilings at Fairwoods. The only grief he brought to me was an appetite that necessitated engaging a wet nurse. My mourning for Far seemed to dry up the milk in my own breasts.

The woman who fed Karsten along with her child was named Bolette. She was a big, coarse girl who had no husband, and the room we prepared for her at the inn soon looked like a magpie's nest. She took no interest in the babies at her udderlike breasts as she slouched in a low chair with spread knees and a blank, ruminative expression on her face. Bolette pleased me because she made no claims on my child.

11

Just when Gammel Hjem was beginning to prosper, financial panic gripped Denmark. Our business dwindled rapidly, and the few guests who did stop with us counted their øre carefully, shunning the bar in their thrift.

Peter remained outwardly cheerful, but I knew he spent long hours worrying over the ledgers when he thought I was asleep. Eventually he sent Mette and Nielsine away because he could not afford to pay them, and I weaned Karsten from Bolette's breast sooner than I might have if the wet nurse's enormous intake of food had not strained our meager supplies. We bought one of Funen's lovely red cows and let her poach in the meadow near the beech woods. No one complained.

Talk of *Amerika* crackled through the town like heat lightning, and letters from those who had claimed the new land's promise were passed from hand to hand until they were limp as old linen.

"Shall we go, Amalie?" Peter said eagerly.

"No, please! I cannot bear to leave Denmark. It is our home. Things will get better."

Karsten cooed and wriggled on the black bear rug at my feet as if to confirm my optimism. A baby in the house can alleviate the grimmest circumstances.

In our recent prosperity Peter had ordered a high-wheeled, canopied perambulator from England, and I would spend hours wheeling Karsten along the delicate serpentine of the Odense River, looking much richer than I felt and wondering what would become of us. Watching the slow skimming of the swans and the comical upending of ducks diving for water bugs, I thought of H. C. Andersen, whose house was nearby. He had transformed hardship to beauty, why couldn't I?

When I came home, I found Peter with pamphlets, books, and newspapers spread over the largest table in the festival room. He looked up, flushed with excitement, as I came in with Karsten on my hip.

"What is all this?" I said.

"Accounts of life in *Amerika*—descriptions, opportunities— there is a place called Shelby County in Iowa where we might go. So many of our people are in Iowa. They say it's better than going to Wisconsin and wearing yourself out cutting trees. Listen to this, Amalie..."

His eyes blazed as he read the words of the poet Christian Winther describing America as a place where it hailed candy and rained lemonade, where roasted squabs flew straight into your mouth, and where country estates were given for the asking. The exuberant hyperbole excited Peter and made him gay, and Karsten, all pink and white gold after his nap in motion, gurgled and crowed as if he understood the fanciful words.

"Will you go, Amalie?"

Through the window I saw the *Dannebrog* flying from a high staff in the town. Its white cross on a blood-red field was stretched between the fingers of the wind, held up like a sign for me.

"No, Peter, I cannot go!"

He clenched his hands and knocked all the papers and books to the floor with one sweep of his arm.

"You are a hard and stubborn woman!" he shouted, stamping out of the inn.

I stopped the violently swinging door and watched him stride toward the beech woods, wanting to run after him with a coat but afraid to approach him until his anger was spent in the walking.

The storm would be over when he came home, I thought, but it wasn't. We lived together in cold courtesy for weeks as the weather grew drear and the winter winds began their perpetual sighing. On the day that Søren Gade told us he was going to America, Peter drained the murky dregs of the Madeira barrel. From then on, we were in a state of cold, silent warfare, and this was how Jonna found us.

She arrived in a hired coach, wrapped to the eyes in smoky fox fur. Peter, thinking that she was a paying guest, hurriedly brushed his neglected clothes and put on a cravat before going out to meet her.

As I watched from the window, Jonna pulled off her gloves and boldly took Peter's face in her mother-of-pearl hands, pressing her lips on his. When they walked toward the inn with their arms twined around each other, they were laughing.

Instead of flying at Jonna with a hatpin as Marie Grubbe would have done, I threw off the drab dress I was wearing and struggled into my best gown of scarlet wool. There was no time for the curling iron, but I piled my hair into a high bun and skewered it with a Spanish comb. Karsten cried for me, but I could not stop to soothe him. I babbled a stream of silly, placating nonsense to him as I upended dresser drawers on the bed in a pawing search for a bottle of scent I never had opened. Taking a few deep breaths to calm myself, I carried Karsten to the door of the festival room.

"Welcome to Gammel Hjem, Jonna. What brings you this way?"

She inspected me coolly before replying, "I have been visiting my family in Korsor, and I thought I would stop to see 'Peter's Folly' for myself."

"Times are bad, though *you* may not know it. When people had money, they spent it here very happily."

"It's pleasant," she said, "like a peasant cottage. Peter always was mad about playing peasant, weren't you, dear Brother-in-law? Remember the garden house at Riisingsminde?"

Peter reddened and said, "That was a long time ago, Jonna."

Jonna raised her hands to arrange her silver-blonde hair. "And that is the child?"

Malice rose in me like the tide. Karsten was wet through, for I had had no time to change him while I was dressing myself, and I plumped him down in Jonna's lean lap, saying, "You must get acquainted with your nephew. His name is Karsten."

She stiffened, raising him above the pearly-gray folds of her merino skirt until Peter took him from her.

"What a spinster you are, Jonna!" He laughed, and she bit her lip, nettled at his teasing.

Jonna stayed for two days, and Peter was profligate with our fast-disappearing woodpile to keep her comfortable in the best guest room. I didn't begrudge her the firewood because I noticed that the warmth she sought from Peter was not forthcoming.

I set a better table than we could afford, and Peter produced a bottle of brandy that our last guest had hidden under the *dyne* and forgotten. The three of us bantered maliciously for those two days, tensely holding our three-cornered balance.

As she was leaving, Jonna made one last effort to reach Peter. She offered to lend him money, and he refused it. Before her carriage was out of sight, Peter and I were headed for our bed. Those days of thrusting and parrying had provided a way of coming back together without humbling ourselves and feeling small.

I grew less tolerant of Peter's squandering so much firewood on Jonna as our woodpile decreased and the cold increased. When I pulled away the logs that covered a nest of red mice and realized how close to the ground the little creatures had built their home, I wished her every kind of bad luck.

One shouldn't do that, for bad luck always comes back to the sender, but while I was scouring the woods for dead branches to burn, it was hard to be charitable.

Peter paid for his gallantry by enduring the cold (which he hated) without complaint, but Karsten and I froze vocally. I draped the black bear rug over Karsten's cradle to keep him warm through the night while Peter and I clung to each other under three *dyner* that exhausted us with their weight.

Each morning Karsten woke us by crying for his milk, and even that didn't satisfy him, for the poor red cow's bones showed now, and the bluish fluid from her udder was not much richer than water. The meadow grass had withered long before, and her daily ration of oats was barely enough to sustain life.

One morning in January, I woke with the unusual feeling that I had had my sleep out. The sun, glinting on the snow outside, was so strong in the room that I knew half the morning must be gone, and I sat up in alarm, pulling the *dyne* from Peter, who complained sleepily at the sudden draft.

The infant cry that could cut through heavy layers of sleep had not sounded, and I sprang from the bed to investigate. Halfway across the icy floor, I stopped and pressed my fists against my mouth. The bear rug was not over the crib, but in it, its hairy border rising from the pale wood like the petals of a malignant flower.

"Peter!"

He bounded from our bed to pull back the robe I could not touch.

"Great God!" He lifted Karsten from the cradle and bent forward over him, sobbing.

Then I was trying to hold them both. Peter and I moved in a macabre waltz in a mad effort to force the warmth of our bodies into the cold, lifeless child between us.

Though I did not want it that way, Karsten was buried among the Jorgen dead at Fairwoods. We chose a tiny, curly cross to mark his grave, but I could not bring myself to have it inscribed *Tak for Alt*. Karsten had not had time to incur a debt of gratitude. Much of a mother's grief when an infant dies consists of thinking of all he might have done and been— the things that will never be.

Karsten was to have taken Far's place in the world, and the double void was such a painful thwarting of restored balance that I stormed heaven for its reason. Locking myself in the pale rose room, I screamed at God, and when I emerged, the household at Fairwoods walked wide around me with a distant, well-bred understanding of my derangement.

Only Frida, my black-and-white magpie, came close. She said little, but when I would toss my head in the senseless motions of grief, she would take my hands and press her sympathy into them.

"But you can't know what it is, Frida, you can't possibly know!"

"I do know, Madame, I once had a child."

"I didn't know you were married."

Turning from me with a mottled blush, she shook her head and spoke in a scarcely audible voice. "No one knows, Madame, please..."

I took her hand, unable to thank her in words for the comfort that had cost her so much.

"Do you think bad of me?" she whispered.

"No—oh no!"

Then I told her of the maids at Gammel Hjem and their superstitious chatter about the name I had given my child. "Can there be anything in it, Frida? Is that why Karsten..."

She would not speak, but her still, frightened face said it all.

"No!" I shouted, "It can't be! I will have another son and name him Karsten to prove it!"

"Oh Madame—" her hands flew up in the pressed palms of prayer.

"Get out!" I screamed.

She ran from the room with the corners of her white apron pressed to her face, and when I next rang for her, she treated me with the same cool respect she showed Jonna and Mathilde. Just one more grief to add to all the others.

Peter tried to stay close to me during those hard days. He refused invitations to ride with Dich and Dines, but sometimes he walked with his father on the frozen drive, and I would watch their grave promenade from the window, wondering what they said to each other. From the back with their heads bent into a wind that billowed their cloaks, they looked alike, but when they turned, Peter seemed the older because of his burdened expression. Less than two years of living with me had been hard on my young husband. He should have married a serene woman like his mother.

As if I had conjured her up, Fru Jorgen spoke softly behind me. "Amalie, you will never forget your first baby, but there will be other children. Living death does no honor to the dead."

I turned, straightening my shoulders. Her arm merely circled me without touching my body, and we moved back to the window to look at our husbands.

"You are young," she said, sweeping her pale lashes over eyes that said more.

I understood and knew that she was right. "When Peter comes in, please tell him that I am upstairs."

He came, chilled through by the wind and the expectation of meeting my sorrow, but when I let my skirt fall in a ring around my feet and stepped out of it to unbutton his coat, we made our own ring of fire that fought back the winter and death itself.

Gradually we came alive to the warmth and comfort of Fairwoods, so different from the cold austerity of our impoverishment at Gammel Hjem, but the price of being warm and well-fed was too high. We were pained by Mathilde's artless maternity. The youngest baby was too much like Karsten, and our hearts curdled as we watched Mathilde kiss the fat folds of his neck or carry him negligently on one hip, unaware of the richness of her privilege.

Under the sightless gaze of the plaster *amorini,* we made such immoderate efforts to replace our lost child that we soon looked like supernatural beings with hollow, burning eyes.

Jonna sensed the striving, and her glances held more

hatred for me and more hunger for Peter. She treated Dich with increasing contempt, disdaining the arm he offered to escort her to the dining room and laughing scornfully at any comment or opinion he expressed.

The crepe wreath on the front door precluded entertaining, and with only the Jorgens at table, barbed words cracked the veneer of formal manners.

"We must go home," Peter said, battered by the hostility of a long meal that boiled dangerously close to an open fight between Jonna and Dich.

"I cannot bear the sight of Gammel Hjem until we know another child is coming!"

"Well, we can't stay here!"

"No."

I could neither go nor stay, and though I despised my indecision, I could not break from it.

It was Dich, finally, who acted. Though I didn't know it at the time, he gave Peter the money to take me to Copenhagen. Suddenly there was money, and I did not question its source, did not know that Dich was buying his peace, such as it was. I thought Peter had sold Gammel Hjem through an agent, for he had spoken of doing so.

Jonna made the astonishing gesture of offering me her fox furs to wear in the city. I was tempted, for they were beautiful—like clouds of pulverized pearls, but if I took them, I would have to bring them back to Fairwoods. Besides, in Jonna's furs, I would not be the self who wanted a new beginning from the green-spired capital, and I must confess that I didn't want Peter reminded of Jonna in any way. I thanked her and told her that my dark green cloak would do well enough.

118

12

Copenhagen still was locked in winter when we arrived. Inch-deep mud in the streets, smoke, fog, and the cacophony of rattling cabs and tram bells colored my first impression of the city. Only when the sun came out on a new snowfall, transforming the capital into a delicate St. Petersburg, did I begin to feel what I had expected to experience the moment I saw Copenhagen—that *hyggelig* or sense of well-being that would strip away an accumulation of sorrows.

Peter grew expansive in the city he knew so well. He wanted to move into more luxurious quarters, but our recent days of poverty had scarred me with caution, and while I was happy to dine in the elegant d'Angleterre on Kongens Nytorv, we stayed on in our cheap rooms in Vesterbrogade.

The neighborhood was plagued by frequent fires, and we would be wakened in the night by a shrill whistle and the cry of *"brand—brand—brand!"* A tub of water stood before every door as a precaution. I made a foolish little paper boat to sail in ours.

Peter and I climbed the spiraling outside stairs of the Church of Our Saviour in a cold, whipping wind for a view of the green spires rising from roofs of tile, slate, and copper. I was sure I could reach out and touch the twisted dragon tails of the Bourse, but as I laughingly tried, I caught a glimpse of the miniature humans far below and clutched Peter's arm in my fear of falling. Still, I did not ask to go down. I was no shepherdess who would pull her chimneysweep from the heights!

For awhile I worried about the money we were spending, but by the time the beeches had leafed in their subtle, green explosion, I was corrupted by luxury. I made no protest when Peter moved us to an expensive hotel near the Raadhus Pladsen. There were new silk dresses in the wardrobe, the dresser top was crowded with cut-glass bottles of French scent, and the first meal sent up to us consisted of *Andesteg Danoise,* champagne, and three-flavored ices sprinkled with crystallized violets.

I never tired of Tivoli Gardens, and Peter indulged me with daily visits to the lovely pleasure park with its oriental-looking pantomime theatre. The loves and adventures of Harlequin and Columbine in the classic Italian pantomime enchanted me. When the curtain closed, the children in the front row would go on calling to Pierrot, "Say something! Say something!" He already had said much to me, this kind, old Pierrot who restored lost situations and put things right again.

Still caught in the illusion of the pantomime, I let Peter steer me into a confectionary.

"You are dreaming awake," he said, "come back to me!"

With the waiter hovering, I could not reply, but I gave Peter a langorous look across the small table, knowing what Jette meant when she had said, "I feel like a rose unfolding." With a sweet sense of power, I realized that I had only to touch his sleeve and we would go back to the hotel, but if we lingered over our chocolate and pastries while the string ensemble played Viennese waltzes, the wanting would only grow stronger. Love watched no clock in Copenhagen.

Peter the Great once drove his carriage up the broad ramp of the Round Tower. Peter Jorgan ran down the same ramp, pulling his wife to the bed of love. I have always believed that our second Karsten was conceived that day.

At any rate, the expected child put an end to the sybaritic game we had been playing for so long, and when Peter left me to look into new business prospects in Jutland, he asked, "Will you be sorry to leave Copenhagen?"

"No," I said truthfully, for I was ready to strive again, "it doesn't matter where I am—I've stored up enough pleasure to last me the rest of my life!"

Peter returned in the most sanguine of spirits. He had bought a general merchandise store in Ribe, using his deed to Gammel Hjem and more of Dich's money for the transaction.

Ribe, the city where Queen Dagmar died; Ribe, the city of many storks; Ribe, whose streets bore the Popish names of the Middle Ages. It was very far from anything I knew.

"Are you displeased?" he said, "You haven't said a word!"

"I was just thinking how strange it will be. I have never been in that part of Jutland."

"It is not as strange as *Amerika!*" he said with an edge in his voice.

"No," I agreed quickly, embracing Ribe in my fear of that greater strangeness, "and I will love it because it will be the birthplace of our child!"

Peter found us a brick house the color of half-ripe mulberries with a marten in the attic to guard against rats, and a temperamental tile stove. Fru Lund, who had lived there all of her long married life, was leaving to make her home with a daughter in Tønder.

Peter insisted on furnishing the parlor with delicate French pieces that he said he could buy cheaply, but I thought the price was still too high. The frugality that had deserted me in Copenhagen was back in full force.

We argued the matter through breakfast, and then Peter changed the subject. "You must go down and see the wreckage the sea storm washed up the fjord! You've never seen anything like it!"

He was right. Brazil nuts, coco-palm, and banana stalks from the tropics were strangely tossed on Danish soil, and as I walked among the exotic debris, I thought of *Dronning Dagmar* anchored in the places from which these things had come. I remembered Liana Hagen and let her calm seep into me.

Her influence was still upon me when I returned home— luckily for Peter. Two men with a dray were unloading furniture in front of our house. French furniture! How clever of him to have got me out of the house while he went against my wishes! My anger grew as I saw it multiplied many times by the gossip mirrors outside the neighbors' windows.

Without the spirit of Liana, Peter and I might have fought in the street, but she would not let me. A strange detachment unhinged my tongue as Peter appeared in our doorway to direct the lifting of a delicate escritoire from the dray.

"Easy with it! Keep it as beautiful as she is." He was infuriatingly pleased with himself, and the men swiveled their heads to stare at me, grinning slowly.

What could I do with a man like that? I could fight his nature and turn coldly from his impracticalities as Mette-Sophie Gade was to do with Gauguin in a later decade, but I knew I would be the poorer for it, so I admired the escritoire and the greenish-blue vitrine with the latticed glass doors.

Grethe Hansen soon appeared to satisfy her curiosity about the new furniture. She pronounced it pretty but too frail. The Hansens were our nearest neighbors and our first friends in Ribe. There is a Danish saying that when three people are gathered, one of them is sure to be called Hansen, and every Danish town must have its Grethe and Lykke Hansen.

My feeling for them danced between affection and exasperation. They provided us with a stodgy social life, which consisted of visiting back and forth in the evenings, making small talk while we ate and drank more than we wanted or needed. The refusal of food was an insult we could not bring ourselves to offer. When we visited in their home, Herr Hansen invariably ended the evening by saying, "Well, Grethe, what to you say? I say when our company goes home, I'm going to bed!"

The first time he did this, I was outraged and couldn't wait to reach the street. "I'll never go back there again!" I sputtered, "I still can't believe such rudeness!"

Peter laughed. "He said it, and I admire him for it. You always know where you are with Lykke Hansen. Would you rather that he strangled his yawns, hating us all the while?"

"I wished myself home hours ago!"

"Let's walk for awhile," Peter suggested, knowing I wouldn't sleep until my indignation faded. "All that eating and sitting makes me feel like a toad!"

We got as far as Greyfriars street before I would admit that I had had enough, and we started back, though Peter wanted to see Domkirken by night.

"I wanted to show you the Devil's private entrance," he said. "On a dark night you must walk around the Cathedral three times, then shout through the keyhole in the cat's head door for the Devil to come out."

"Peter, why would anyone want to see the Devil?"

He shrugged with a deep chuckle. "Who knows? To make a Faustian pact, perhaps, or to complain about the poor quality of one's temptations. Anyhow, it makes a charming story. When you go to the market with Grethe tomorrow, have her take you to Domkirken. You must see the sights of Ribe while you are able to appear on the streets."

I chafed at the thought of being cooped up by advancing pregnancy. It was getting too warm for my heavy, full cloak, but perhaps I could find some shapeless garment of linen. I spoke of this to Peter, telling him that he should sell such things in the store. Pregnant women would be his most grateful customers.

"It is not done," he said, rejecting the idea without considering it seriously.

Grethe and I did go to Domkirken, and she was uneasy the whole time we were inside, certain that the heavy overlay of Popery would corrupt her. The cat's head door filled her with such powerful dread that she covered her eyes when we passed it.

"It's broad daylight, Grethe! Even if the legend were true, we would be quite safe."

"You be careful what you say!" she snapped, looking around as if she expected the Devil himself to be listening.

The cathedral portraits were full of life, almost racy, and I stood for long minutes before the painting of a self-satisfied lady with two husbands. She smiled like a cat in a dairy!

We saw less of the Hansens after Peter met some young teachers from the Latin school and brought them home for evenings of talk and music. Peter had great respect for educators, but he also had illusions of creating a salon, and the idea amused me.

I particularly liked Andreas Christensen, who came from the island of Fanø just off our western coast. He wore a perpetually mournful expression, but when he took his violin from its melon-shaped case, he coaxed laughter from it. He played whenever I asked except on days when he had been forced to cane a student. Corporal discipline violated his gentle spirit so harshly that he would not recover for days.

His friend Gustav, who taught the younger boys, tried to pull Andreas from his gloom by clowning and reciting poetry, but it was useless. Only time could erase that melancholy.

Gustav Bartholsen was never anything but himself. He was an uncomplicated, lazy boy who was taken on at the Latin School because his father and the headmaster had been lifelong friends. He wenched and drank heavily without conscience and bragged about it.

When I scolded him, he would answer with mock humility, "Yes, Mor, you're quite right, Mor! I must try to be more like Andreas, the model pedagogue!"

Each could have used some qualities of the other, and I was fond of them both. I thought I wanted them to marry and be happy, but when they brought girls to meet me, I always found something wrong with their Karens and Maries. When the boys asked for my opinion later, I would damn with faint praise or sink a tiny barb of objection in my compliments.

"She seems pleasant enough, but what can she talk about?"

"She must be a good cook. She looks like a dumpling herself!"

I had planned a special party to celebrate Andreas' birthday. Though my time was very near, I thought I could reign in my own parlor in one of the loose tents I had fashioned for myself. In the early afternoon I felt the low, dull back pain that signals the outset of labor, but the whole business had taken so long the first time that I decided to go ahead with the evening.

The boys arrived with out-of-season flowers in paper frills, we drank Andreas' health, and he played for us without too much urging. As the pains came closer together, I called Peter into the next room and asked him to bring the doctor.

He nodded toward Gustav and Andreas. "Shall I send them away?"

"No, don't spoil Andreas' party. Give them some more brandy and tell them they can stay until the doctor comes. I don't want to be alone in the house."

This was the shortest period of labor I was ever to know. The child was in a frenzy to be born, and I could not wait for the doctor. The great contractions engulfed me, and when my fearfully exploring hand touched the child's wet hair, I screamed.

Gustav took one look at all the blood and was sick in the chamber pot, but Andreas ran back for his violin bow and tore a string from it to tie the cord. He seemed to know what to do. His shaking hands worked quickly, and then he was holding the slippery, bloody infant by its heels and whacking the mucus from its throat.

When Peter arrived with the doctor, young Karsten was sleeping in the beech wood cradle and I was fighting to stay awake on clean linens that Andreas had found somehow.

When Doctor Lervad complimented Andreas on a fine delivery, the young school master muttered, "I didn't know it would be like that—all that blood and pain—" then he fled, trying to roll down his bloody shirt cuff with the hand that held his ruined bow.

I wanted to call out my thanks, but my tongue was too thick. He would be back to see the child who shared his birthday, and I would tell him then. I fell asleep with my hand in Peter's, grateful that we had a son once more.

The women of the neighborhood came to call with the precious "loved up" plants from their window sills, for frost had pinched the last of the late garden flowers. They admired Karsten, remarking on his strong lungs and on the small fists that curled with such determination. He was a fine baby, but not as perfect as the other Karsten. This one was redder and darker-haired. Still, he made me glad.

Andreas would come any day, I thought, he would want to see the child he had brought into the world. But I was wrong. Andreas never came back to our house, not even when I wrote him a note scolding him for neglecting us.

Gustav came, though, and he was strangely evasive about Andreas. When I pressed him, he told me that Andreas had gone home to Fanø. I would not let the matter rest and begged Peter to find out why. I wish I hadn't.

Andreas had cut off his testicles with a razor blade, fainted, and nearly bled to death before he was found. All he would say was that he would never cause a woman such pain—he had seen to it!

All through the years this has lain buried in the silt of my heart like a cold, gray stone.

13

When our second Karsten was just learning to walk, Mor came to visit us in Ribe. Though she had aged considerably, widowhood became her. In her black alpaca gowns and severe bonnets, she cast an impressive reflection in the gossip mirrors along our street.

She brought the news that my real mother was ailing, and the doctors did not know what was sapping her strength. Also that my brother Ib, whom I'd never seen, had written of his life among the Mormons in Salt Lake City, describing the Lion House where Brigham Young established his many wives.

Grethe Hansen was scandalized by the tales of Mormon polygamy, but she was avid to hear more, and she was not above joking about it.

"I must have Lykke bring home some women," she said, laughing. "One for scrubbing, one to bake, and another to market while I sit in the parlor with my feet on a cushion!"

Bouncing Karsten on my knees, I said, "I wouldn't mind the others during the day, but the nights would drive me mad!"

"You are very free with your tongue, Amalie!" Mor reproved, "And do put more clothes on that baby! His little legs are turning blue!"

"It's summer!" I protested, but Karsten sneezed, vindicating Mor, and I swathed him like a mummy to avoid further contention.

There is something comfortable about woman talk in a kitchen where pots boil gently and clocks tick without anxiety; where a baby takes his first reeling steps from one table leg to another. This is a safe world where talk of death, disease, and change cannot alarm, for there is strength to bear all in the community of women. I had no way of knowing how soon I would need this strength.

Just as he was walking into life, our Karsten was taken from it. A little sneeze, then a skin hot to the touch, and finally a frightening rattle in the chest that came on him so quickly that Dr. Lervad could do nothing to save him.

Peter drove me to the sea to gather ocean-smoothed stones to make a border for the tiny grave.

"You have not cried, Amalie," he said gently, "it would be better if you did."

I walked close to the foam breaking on the sand and would have kept on walking if Peter had not pulled me back roughly, wrenching my shoulder. The pain pulled me from my numbness, and I began to reason coldly.

I had defied superstition by naming both of my babies Karsten. I had been punished for it. Whoever controlled these things should be told that I would not do it again. God would not kill my babies, and whom did that leave but the Devil himself?

That night when Peter was safely asleep, I slipped out of bed and peeled off the nightgown I had put over my clothes. Wrapping myself in a long, dark cloak, I let myself out noiselessly and hurried toward Domkirken.

I passed the old man who cried the hours and heard him sing out in a cracked voice, "One o'clock on a foggy morn— Sweet Jesus keep the innocent—"

"The innocent are dead!" I hissed, running from the sound of his voice.

Three drunken students stumbled over the cobbles singing about a "maiden with golden hair—'n angel s' fair—" and when I tried to slip past, one of them caught my arm and brought my face close to his. I nearly choked in fumes of akvavit as I struggled with him. His grip was too strong to break until I bit his hand and left him howling.

Out of breath from running, I stood outside the cat's head door and tried to spit out the filthy, raw taste of the student's hand. The akvavit must have worked out through his skin.

"On a dark night," Peter had said. Surely this night was dark enough. I couldn't make out the keyhole through which I was to shout, and the blackness seemed to weigh on my face.

I would have welcomed the beneficent ghost of Queen Dagmar said to walk the streets of Ribe, and I thought of her lying on her deathbed ringed by "all the ladies that in Denmark were," pleading for King Valdemar, who was eighty miles away in Skanderborg. Queen Dagmar died as the King rode up the street, but he begged the prayers of all present that he might take his leave of her, and Dagmar revived. Fixing her bloody red eyes on him, she pleaded with him not to marry Berengeria after her death, then told him goodbye. What power the brown-haired Berngerd must have had to make Valdemar gainsay Dagmar's dying wish! How little respect for a miracle he showed in making the Portuguese princess his queen!

Almost hoping to meet the shade of the yellow-haired queen, I circled Domkirken once rapidly. If I saw her, it would be a sign that I did not have to call on the Dark Prince. She did not appear. The second trip around was slower, and when I neared the end of the third circling, my steps dragged and my heart pounded.

My hands shook as they traced the cat's head, and when I cried, "Beelzebub, come out!" my voice was so weak that I scarcely could expect results. I tried again, "Satan, come out!"

Nothing happened, and I went on shouting until I was nearly hysterical. The noise I made didn't bring the Devil, but a policeman came. Apparently he was used to people shouting for the devil, because the scolding he gave me was half-humorous, and he escorted me home with the greatest courtesy.

At our door, he smilingly touched his hat. "You gave me a turn, Madame; for a moment I thought you were the Sunrise Maiden herself!"

Peter did not stir when I came back to bed, and I lay awake beside him for hours, terrified and ashamed to pray to God after I had tried to speak with the Adversary. Toward morning, I threw myself on His mercy, praying recklessly. Then I cried, and Peter woke to comfort me with the solid realities of the flesh. It is not altogether a bad thing to know that the Devil does not want to see you.

That April, a pair of storks chose our rooftop for their nest.

"They never would come to Fru Lund," Grethe Hansen marveled, "but you deserve some good fortune after so much sadness. There will be no death in this house for a year, and where the stork builds his nest, no lightning will strike."

I was not afraid of lightning, for we did not live under thatch, but I was glad for a respite from death.

Three times it snowed on the big cartwheel nest, which is the best of omens. Since my scorn of superstition had been so severely chastened, I cherished the dignified, red-legged birds that were to bring me luck.

The Danish church, both before and after the Reformation, was not zealous about uprooting small, harmless paganisms. The church fathers considered them good palliatives for the harshness of life.

Putting my pride aside, I no longer spurned superstitions as crutches for the weak. I quietly embraced the notions that gave me comfort, though I did not tell Peter, for I was afraid he would laugh at me. He walked a tightrope between the age of reason and the later romanticism, taking what he liked from both.

Once I heard him tell Gustav, "You can allow yourself to be sentimental only as long as you are aware of being so."

"But if you know it, you will bring irony to bear," Gustav pointed out, "and then your condition no longer can be described as sentimental."

"Just so," Peter said; "the whole business adds up to a pleasant game!"

The summer passed quietly, and by the time the storks flew back to Egypt, I knew that I was pregnant again. I was reading *Heaven and Its Wonders and Hell* by Emanuel Swedenborg when I discovered my condition, and I pinned wrapping paper over the thin section on Hell to avoid marking the baby with such baneful literature.

Reading that little children were cared for by angel women in Heaven, I was glad that my baby boys were in good hands, happy and garlanded with flowers, but those angel women would not have the next one!

As Christmas approached, Danish-Americans appeared in Ribe to fan the emigrant fever with their talk of business opportunities and high profits in a place called Iowa. Peter was ready to board the next ship. I didn't argue with him this time—not with words. I merely took his hand and placed it on my swelling body.

"Can you feel the small Dane?"

On New Year's Eve, I used the pile of broken crockery around our door to point out how successful Peter had been in Ribe. On this night, Danes shatter dishes against the doors of those they esteem, and Peter's many customers had done him proud with the chipped dishes from their cupboards. Every time we rose from our traditional dinner of boiled cod and mustard sauce to give sweets and money to the New Year's pirates who rang our bell, I took admiring notice of the growing mound of shards.

Peter had to admit that the business was prospering, and when I was satisfied that his attack of emigrant fever had passed, I put my mind to arranging a perfect New Year's Day. Grethe Hansen insisted that whatever one does on New Year's, one will do all year long, and I was determined not to be bound to any uncongenial activity for a year.

As we began our round of New Year's calls, I told Peter that he would have to go alone to the house of Herr Barrit, a rude, dyspeptic supplier of salt fish. I would see only the people I liked on this first day of the year.

"You are my wife, and you will go with me!"

I started to rebel, then took thought and agreed to accompany him. Seeing the Barrits or someone like them every day of the new year would be better than fighting with Peter daily.

Laura was born at the height of the spring flowering. I was sure that I would not have named a third boy Karsten, but I was glad that I wasn't put to the test.

Visiting neighbors surrounded Laura with such huge armsful of blossoms that we called her our *blomster pige,* our flower girl. She was a pale rose with eyes as deeply blue as Venetian glass, and our storks had come back to assure us that we could keep her at least for a year.

After three years, she was still with us, growing beautifully. Peter doted on her to the exclusion of good sense. On a buying trip to Paris, he purchased a tiny violin for her from a dwarf street musician who swore the instrument was a genuine Stradivarius. He was cheated, of course, but he didn't care.

He wanted to take Laura to the sun—to Italy or to the South of France—but I insisted that she was too young for such rigorous travel. Worse yet, he wanted to give her America like an oyster on a half-shell.

"You have seen to it that she was born a Dane," he argued, "now give her *Amerika* to grow in!"

"Look at her," I said, yearning over the sweet seriousness of her small face as she put her doll to bed in a shallow drawer of the escritoire, "could she be more perfect? She does not need *Amerika!*"

That whole summer seemed like a festival to me. The days were long and soft, and we enjoyed the white nights of *Holme* Week late in July when the hay was in and people reveled with a sense of earned pleasure on the stretch of green marshland that King Erik Menved had given to Ribe in the Middle Ages.

One morning in August, Peter decided that Laura must experience a fair. We set out gaily, stopping the carriage some distance from the tents and gay banners to keep the horses from shying at the noise of firecrackers.

Keeping a bonnet on Laura was impossible. To keep her tiny, pink face from toasting, I would have had to make a black mask for her like those worn by the women of Fanø to protect their complexions when they worked in the fields.

Laura loved the excitement and took the smiles of strangers as her due. Peter bought her decorated sweetheart cakes and hoisted her to his shoulders to watch a troupe of performing acrobats.

Hearing a tune in a shifting minor, I wandered off to listen to a troubadour who had collected a rapt audience. The singer's voice rose above the noises of the fair like oil on water.

Proudly o'er the ocean waves
sped the steamer Austria.
Passengers it had in numbers
Going to Amerika.
To the captain who commanded
Never dream came of the blow
Which fate for him upon this voyage
Unluckily prepared had. . .

I started to turn away, but somehow I could not go. I stayed to listen to the horrors of fire on shipboard: women throwing their children over the side, then being swallowed up by red and yellow flames. The listeners gasped in sympathy, and when the last note faded, the troubadour passed his hat. I dropped a few *øre* into it and stumbled away, shaken.

When I found Peter and Laura again, my distress lessened. I could not speak of the terrible song I had heard, so I searched for a normal commonplace. "Who is in the store today, Peter?"

"Crazy Andrew."

Peter had insisted that hiring this strange, old man to do odd jobs and occasionally wait on a customer was an act of social imagination, but I thought it impractical. Crazy Andrew carved weird images in wood and gave them away. Small boys ran after him in the streets and jeered at him. Who would buy from such a person?

"I know what you're thinking," Peter said, "but it is such a fine day that few customers will come. If they don't find what they want, let them come back tomorrow. I don't care if we don't make one *krone* today!"

"Oh well, Annelise can manage him."

Peter might have let it go at that, but he never took advantage of my misunderstandings. He said, "Annalise is meeting her young man, Hans wanted to fish, and Thorval needed to fix some broken tiles on his roof—but I tell you, it will be all right!"

I tried to believe him, but the song about the steamer *Austria* had opened the door to all kinds of apprehensions, and I had an unpleasant feeling about Crazy Andrew being in charge at the store that nagged at me most of the afternoon.

We came home at sunset, weary as the streams of pilgrims who had passed through Ribe in medieval times. I was holding the sleeping weight of Laura while Peter unlocked the door, and we planned to go straight to bed, but we did not sleep that night.

Lykke Hansen came running with Grethe close behind him. Their breathless shouts mingled until the only word I could distinguish was *brand!*

A fire had started in the store, and Crazy Andrew did not call for help until it was raging beyond control. The fire wagons could do no more than save the adjoining buildings. Apparently Crazy Andrew had set his lighted pipe too close to a pile of shavings from his carving when he went to serve a customer. He was beating the flames with his coat when they carried him forcibly from the building.

Peter was back in the carriage before the Hansens stopped talking, and I thrust Laura into Grethe's arms to run after him.

Blocks from the store, we drove into deep pools of water from the fire-fighting. The horses fought the reins as Peter drove them deeper into a pall of smoke.

The store was unrecognizable. Only the doorposts stood

above piles of blackened brick, and what had been the floor was piled waist-high with ruined merchandise—bolts of cloth half-eaten by flame, blackened copper, kid boots shriveled by the heat, and a big doll with a cracked porcelain face.

Peter started to get down from the carriage, then sat back. "What's the use? Everything is gone."

The hollow hopelessness of his voice frightened me until I saw him set his jaw.

"We can start again," I suggested almost fearfully. Perhaps it was too soon for him to hear what he already knew.

He turned the horses decisively. "Yes, but not here."

"Where, then?"

"I think you know, Amalie. I will go first and make a place for you."

I was beaten, and I knew it. The paper boat in the Vester-brogade water tub and the steamer *Austria* gyrated in the whirlpools of my mind. *Brand! Brand! Brand!*

"All right, Peter, let us go to *Amerika*."

14

We had planned to say goodbye in Ribe. Peter wanted to go home to Funen before sailing to America from Copenhagen, and my mother's condition demanded that I hurry to Stilbjerg with Laura to nurse her until Peter sent for us.

The day before we were to part, the enormity of the separation struck me so forcibly that I begged Peter to let us stay with him as long as he was on Danish soil. I convinced myself that my mother's illness was exaggerated.

We spent a few days at Fairwoods which enabled me to remember Peter's home with more pleasure than I could have done otherwise. Laura made the difference, perhaps. She enchanted her grandparents and her uncles, and even Jonna viewed her as something of an achievement.

Jonna had grown thinner, and while she still was beautiful, the hard, bright flame of her discontent was firing her to a porcelain lifelessness. Jonna was the stuff of Henrik Ibsen's future female characters, and like them, she was bent on destroying herself. I approached her with a wary pity which she turned aside.

As we continued our journey toward Copenhagen, I took

Laura into Roskilde Cathedral and led her to the tomb of Queen Margrethe beneath the high-vaulting arches of pale red brick. Seeing the calm, alabaster face I had imagined for so long, I was speechless, but Laura said, "Why does she sleep in her clothes, Mor?"

Absorbed in the serene face, I had not even noticed the Queen's stiffly formal medieval robes, and I answered absently, "Because she is a queen."

"I don't want to be a queen, then. I like to go to bed in my nightshift—it's soft!"

"There are better things than comfort," I said, but she didn't hear me, for the ancient clock was striking the hour and St. George was attacking the dragon on the little platform jutting from the wall beyond the main entrance.

I held the image of Queen Margrethe's face through the days that followed, and it helped me let Peter go. His ship, the steamer *Glasgow*, looked sturdy and seaworthy, but still I was afraid, and if I had not had Laura to comfort, I would have pulled him back from the gangplank with tearful pleadings.

He stood above us on a high deck, looking more distinguished, I thought, than the other emigrants. I forced myself to smile and wave, but Laura howled and tried to break away from me to run to him. I carried her off the dock before the ship sailed, explaining that one must never watch a loved one out of sight. When we heard the departing whistle from the restaurant where I had taken her for chocolate and cakes, I closed my eyes and held my breath.

When we arrived in Stilbjerg, I found my mother sicker than I had expected her to be. Bedfast, she was propped up with many bolsters, and when Laura ran to her and fell against her elbow, she screamed with pain.

"My joints burn with the Devil's own fire!" she moaned,

then touched Laura's cheek gently, "but it is not your fault, *lille pige.* Sit carefully beside Bedstemor."

She would not live long, I thought. Maybe she would be gone before Peter was ready for us, and then we would be strangers in this bleak, little village where there seemed to be no young people or children.

I did the best I could for my mother, administering a bewildering variety of medicines the doctor had prescribed and brewing the strong tea that eased her pain. She warned me not to drink it myself, for it contained opium.

When she was eased, her mind wandered, dissolving time in its ramblings from childhood to the recent past.

"Mor, do not blame Karsten!" she would cry out. "Hansine has bewitched him!"

"How?" I asked carefully, hoping to pass for my own grandmother until I had an answer, but the vibrations of my voice caused an odd shifting behind her eyes and she became the busy matron worrying about the lard rendering which must be done immediately.

"The fat will go rancid if we don't get at it before sunup! Are the kettles ready? And is there wood?"

"Yes, yes, everything is here."

Laura ran into the room, begging to play on the heath, and my mother raised up in wild-eyed protest, "No! Never go there!"

I thought it just as well to keep her away from the tawny hills with their pools of swamp. She might drown or be bitten by the adders that glide under the heather.

Time passed with hypnotic languor as we waited for Peter to establish himself in the new land. The heath was a calendar that turned its own pages with excruciating deliberation. The purple heather carpet browned imperceptibly and the leaves of the stunted oaks curled to maroon claws at such a sluggish pace that I thought the year was standing still. And so I waited: for my mother to die, for my reunion with Peter, and for the birth of another child.

How I missed Peter's touch! I imagined it so strongly that I looked for marks on my skin and was surprised to find none. His letters spoke boldly of such matters, but I could not bring myself to reply in kind. What if my letter should fall into other hands?

My mother could tell me so much if her mind were clear, but the opium floated her to incoherence, then sleep, and I hadn't the heart to withhold it from her.

One day while I was boiling sago for sweet soup, she cried from her bed, "Amalie! Bring her back, Karsten, it is wrong to hurt me so!"

I stopped stirring with the long wooden spoon to listen, and as the sago boiled over, raising billows of steam, I pushed the kettle back with my bare hands. I scarcely felt the burning pain as I strained to hear what she was saying.

"Karsten—I told you what I did with the pastor because I trusted you, my brother, and you said it was no worse than yourself and Hansine—and now you cut my heart out for an old sin?"

What was this, the moldy Lazarus of an old guilt rising to mock Far's fairy tale? I shook her roughly, mingling my pain and hers. "When did this happen?" I shouted, "Whose child am I?"

A great tremor went through her, dispelling her phantoms. She spoke clearly and rationally. "Why shouldn't you know the truth? You are Niels Ibsen's child, and I let my brother take you to spare my dear Niels a greater pain. Before I ever knew him, I went to the heath with the pastor—innocently, but I did not come back innocent. Karsten knew and kept my secret and used it against me when he wanted a child of his own blood—"

"Oh, why didn't you keep me? My father would have loved you still!"

"Niels could not have borne the knowing. He was a proud man. The first helping of a woman's heart is her husband's!"

My mother wept then, and so did I.

Far was dead, and I could not bring myself to think ill of him. I collected the shards of my fairy tale for mending, for the truth alone was too barren a possession.

When the heath began to struggle from the foggy *dyne* of winter, Peter's summons arrived.

"I have a house, not so fine as any you know of, but shelter enough. I had wanted more for you, but I cannot wait. The steamer *Agrippa* sails from Copenhagen March 15. Come!"

I looked up from the letter to meet my mother's suffering gaze and knew I could not leave her while she lived.

The *Agrippa* sailed without us while Peter fretted in a foreign town called Harlan. The longer we waited, the more heavily pregnant I would be for the crossing.

Across that frightening infinity of water lay the America I now longed for. Peter's descriptions of the shoulder-high prairie grass, the groves of trees beside small streams, and the fertile land glowed in my mind, and his face was in the foreground.

First I prayed that God would release my mother from pain, but when her condition struck a plateau of misery, less worthy solutions occurred to me. Who would know if I gave her too much opium? I would, and I couldn't live with the knowledge. Why couldn't an adder from the heath glide into her bed and stop the poor heart with its venom? She had embraced a human adder on that same heath in her youth, and the poison was with us still. These thoughts frightened me, but the harder I tried to turn them away, the more persistent they became.

Finally she worsened. I asked if I should send for the pastor, and she threw her head back against the bolsters in a violent refusal.

"I'd go to Hell first!"

I tried to calm her with Luther's doctrine of the priesthood of the believer.

"Yes," she nodded, "that's the way it is. I will stand before the God who made me and tell Him how it was."

"He knows," I said, "and He has forgiven you long ago."

She reached out her arms and pulled my face close to hers. I could feel the swollen joints of her fingers at the back of my neck. They burned.

"Amalie—" she gasped—"you are so good . . ."

And with that mistaken pronouncement, she died.

With a great, shuddering sigh I unlocked her fingers and sent Laura into the weak spring sun to play while I scrubbed the room and hung it with white, readying it for the calls of the few ancients who had known my mother.

I hired two men to dig her grave, not in the churchyard, but on the heath. They charged me double, partly for the harder work, and partly because they thought I was doing wrong. I thought otherwise. In her mind, the church was the human machinery that obscured God, and I wanted her free from it at last, cleanly committed to the heather and on her own with Him.

After long deliberation, I had *Tak for Alt* cut into a curly cross for my mother. Much of her life had been hard and sad, but it was human, and that was something to be thankful for.

PART THREE

Land of the Lemonade Rain

146

15

There are land Danes and sea Danes, according to an old saying, and before our ship, the *Sangviniker*, slid from the Copenhagen dock, I was convinced that I was a land Dane. Even in the crush of ascending the gangplank, I felt the wild urge to run back to firm ground, but the name of the ship, "The Optimist," shamed me into controlling myself.

Laura and I were among the first to board, for no one had come to see us off. Mor was the only one who might have come, but she was sick in Ausig and could not travel to Zealand. Perhaps it was just as well, for I was not sure I could face her with what I now knew.

The leave-takings were painful. Old women said goodbye to their sons, never expecting to see them again. Sweethearts tore apart, only to rejoin in an agony of intensity, unwilling to let any kiss be the last. Families that had exhausted all words of farewell wore graveside expressions as they waited for the numb suspension to end, but when the gangplank was raised, essential messages rose in the voices of Babel.

My only farewell was to the spires of Copenhagen, which I had loved. I held Laura high, commanding her to remember the sight of the city, but she was more interested in the children playing tag around stacks of coiled rope, the unloading of coal from English vessels, and the strange, hollow-sounding speech of Dutchmen mingling with streams of musical Italian.

I wondered whether my household goods had been loaded in the hold. I hadn't brought much, just two cane-seated chairs from my mother's house as remembrances, a walnut dresser that no one in Ribe had wanted to buy, the cast iron pans for making *Æbleskiver,* the apple pancakes Peter loved, and four feather *dyner.* Our clothes, except for those we would need on the voyage, were in an ironbound oak chest.

I stopped a tall sailor with a reddish-blond beard and asked about my things.

He said, "All is aboard, Madame. You will be able to start again like Noah after the flood."

"Are you quite sure?

"We have not closed the hatch. Come and see for yourself."

I peered into the tightly packed hold, dizzied by the sight of the familiar objects of so many lives crowded together in an impersonal intimacy. Besides the furniture and chests, there were plants with roots bound into rich, Danish earth. There were fruit trees, lily bulbs, and rose bushes. I could not see my own things and had to take their presence on faith, for I could not ask for more assurance.

Soon there was a commotion in the corridors. The steerage passengers were streaming upward for a last look at the homeland as we passed Helsingør. Laura and I joined the mob, fighting impolitely for space at the rail. I let my cloak fall back to show my condition in the hope that someone would give us a place, and a red-cheeked farm boy obliged. We found our view obstructed by the fog that blunted the outlines of Kronborg Castle's Flemish turrets. I wanted to tear the mist away to possess this one last image in clarity. It was as if Denmark hid her face to keep from watching us out of sight.

"*Farvel, Holger Danske,*" I said, and Laura asked why I was crying. How could I tell her that I was saying goodbye to a legend and that the land where we were going had no Holger Danske to rise and defend it in time of need?

The stormy passage stretched the voyage of the *Sangviniker* to eighteen days. We would not arrive when Peter expected us, and I was afraid that I could not let him know in time. I could not bear to think of his disappointment in that strange, faraway railroad station in Iowa.

On the last day of the voyage, we dressed in our best clothes and crowded the decks early in the morning to catch our first glimpse of the new world. The accordion and fiddles of the deck musicians were silent as we stood in quiet groups gazing at the western horizon. Then New York City seemed to rise from the sea like Atlantis reappearing. Glinting gold, mauve, and pink in the morning sun, the panorama of the city was a diamond point etching. It was hard and male in its power; nothing like the feminine cities of Denmark.

A woman's voice began the old Norwegian hymn, "On this our festal day..." Other voices took it up, and we sang it through as the *Sangviniker* came slowly up through the narrows.

"I'm coming, Peter, I'm coming!" I murmured.

The five-day train journey seemed longer than the eighteen days on the ocean. I was drowning in a vastness of land that made my Denmark of the many islands seem a toy country. When I thought the green beauty of New York must stretch to infinity, I was faced with the mountains of Pennsylvania with valleys so deep that I grew dizzy looking into them. All that wild, tangled land so wastefully uncultivated made me hungry for man's mark on the soil. Without the boundaries I craved, the self I knew seemed to spill out and get lost.

Laura took the strangeness in her stride. A young child accepts the new as normal and would not be surprised to see a man walking on the ceiling or palm trees in the Arctic. She expected to find Peter waiting in a house like the one we had left in Ribe, unchanged by the threatening power to shape that I sensed in America.

The last day was the longest, and Peter's face was so clearly before me that I thought I was seeing double as he ran beside the still moving train to board it and embrace us where we sat.

Laura had just wakened, and she said matter-of-factly, "Hello, Papa—" Then she remembered where she was and what was happening. She gave a little shriek and covered his face with kisses.

Above her feverishly bobbing head, Peter's eyes locked with mine, and their intensity dizzied me. He put Laura off his lap, and we clung, speechless and trembling.

"Oh, my love!" he said hoarsely, "Welcome! Welcome to America!"

"Peter, you look—younger!"

He laughed and broke from my arms to attend to the luggage. What blessedness it was to be taken care of once more!

A gentle rain was falling as we stepped from the train, and I teasingly thrust my tongue out. "Well, Peter, it doesn't taste like lemonade to me!"

"Taste it again!"

Just then the rain stopped, and soon the sun broke through to dance on the wet, green exuberance that sprang from virgin soil.

"You will love this place, Amalie," Peter said, "I will make it rain lemonade for you!"

16

The dwellings I had seen on the overland train journey did not prepare me for the house that was to be my home. Situated across the railroad tracks from the flour mill, it consisted of three small rooms, and its exterior was unpainted. It looked raw, like a loaf of bread taken from the oven too soon, and it exuded the harsh but not unpleasant odor of pine.

"I know it is not what you expected, Amalie," Peter said, "but a house like this is no disgrace here. Until you have been in Harlan for five years, you belong to a freemasonry of the poor with possibilities. If you are still poor after that time, you are considered shiftless."

With Laura on his hip, he led me inside, and I saw that packing boxes were the chief furnishings of the rooms. A fringed spread of garnet red had been thrown over a long box to make a setee, and crates that still bore the heavy black lettering of shipping addresses were the chairs around an oak table that was the only manufactured piece I could see.

The small kitchen was nearly filled by a black stove big enough to receive sacrifices to Baal, and a bed with a towering headboard choked the room where we would sleep. Peter set

Laura down to pull out the trundle that was to be hers.

"You have things very clean," I said, trying to find something to appreciate.

"Lily Hertert, one of my customers, lent me her woman to get things ready for you. Mrs. Hertert left a present for you in the kitchen."

I went to look, and there was a bag of fine, white sugar propped against a vase of wild roses. Peter found me weeping over it and held me, not asking why I cried. I probably couldn't have told him that in my great weariness, uncertainty, and bewilderment, the kindness of a stranger could produce tears.

Laura quickly claimed the rooms, then went outside to listen to the high humming of the flour mill. Alone, we both started to talk at once, for there was so much to tell. In spite of my exhaustion, I knew I could not rest until I had spilled the feelings hoarded through the long months of separation and journeying.

Peter was eager to tell me about this new town, which he loved with the inexplicable passion a man can feel for an ugly woman.

"Think, Amalie, Harlan is only two years older than you! I have never known a place so new! Here we are all equal—we can lift and build together! And look at you—soon we will see what you and I have made together!"

Not soon enough, I thought. My body was too heavy for love, but the hunger was there for both of us, and we were almost relieved when Laura ran to us with a tight bundle of wild roses in her scratched hands.

"She brings us the symbol of fertility," Peter said, "we will surpass Christian IV yet! But come now, let me show you the chickens. I bought them today, and they are beautiful!"

I admired the buff-colored laying hens with their bright, inscrutable eyes, then made a quick meal with the provisions Peter had supplied and fell across the bed in my traveling clothes, not to waken until morning.

When I struggled from heavy sleep, my skin was covered with itching, red welts, and though Peter was cursing in English, I caught the full import of his words. Laura was disfigured by the red welts too. I rolled back the mattress and searched for the vermin I was sure we had picked up on the journey, though I couldn't imagine why the filthy things hadn't bitten us before.

I could find nothing. The heavy muslin sheets exuded the strong scent of lye soap, which should have repelled any crawling creature. I spent the whole day airing and boiling garments and went to bed with the exhausted certainty that the Jorgen household was purged of pests.

Less tired than the night before, I slept fitfully, imagining stinging sensations, and in the morning the three of us had a new crop of welts.

"This is terrible!" Peter said, "I'll go and find Doctor Gus. This could be a disease we don't know about!"

He strode off toward the meager business section on the planks that served as sidewalks, and before I had finished the breakfast dishes, he was climbing out of the doctor's one-horse rig and tying the reins to the crude hitching post he had pounded into the ground in front of our house.

The doctor was a short, powerfully built man with the studied tangle of curls seen on Roman statuary. He missed nothing with the amber-bright eyes under bushy brows.

He said "Good morning" in Danish and reached for my welted arm. The greeting was all the Danish he knew, and Peter translated as he said, "This place is too clean for bugs. Maybe it's hives. What have you been eating?"

We told him, and then Peter groaned as we were ordered to

eat nothing but bread and milk until further notice. Doctor Gus laughed, reaching into his worn leather satchel for a bottle of green-brown liquid that was to relieve the itching.

"You'll be needing me for something else before long," he said, glancing at the bulge of my sacklike apron. Then he patted Laura's cheek and went out to yank the reins from the post and drive away.

"He has been up all night, Peter told me, "I caught him just as he was reaching for his nightshirt, he said. Now I must go to the store. If I'm not there before Edward comes, he calls me a lazy Dane!"

"There is no such thing!" I snorted. "Shall I send food with you?"

"I will walk to you when I am hungry." He made a face. "Bread and milk! That is something to look forward to!"

Peter had told me of Edward Parmeter, his partner in the store, praising the man's business sense and personal qualities. Parmeter was the youngest son of a wealthy Virginia family, and according to Peter, his manners were fine enough for the Dresden china court of Copenhagen.

I was both eager and reluctant to meet Parmeter and the other friends Peter had made; eager because I wanted to share as much of Peter's life as possible, reluctant because I was locked in my own language and could not speak to his friends. At least I could look, intuit, and judge by everything but the spoken word, but even that would have to wait until after the baby was born.

I quailed at the thought of learning English. It would mean the re-making of my soul, for one does not know a language until the emotions can move in it. From the English I had heard, I considered the language an inhospitable womb for the feelings.

That day stretched long. I fed the chickens, dusted and

swept the three rooms, and smeared the nasty-smelling liquid on Laura and me. Peter had left the *Dannevirke*, the Danish language newspaper from Cedar Falls, on the dining room table. I sat down with it and soon was engrossed by a serialized portion of Tolstoy's *Anna Karenina*. Never having read the novel, I had no idea how it had begun, but the section available to me held my attention, and I was impatient to know what the next installment would bring. Perhaps Anna's husband would stop being so impossible and everything would end well.

I had just turned to a piece titled "Across the Glaciers of Greenland" when Laura came in pulling someone after her. I stood clumsily, blushing at being caught reading in the middle of the morning.

"Mor, she lives in the big house," Laura said, pointing to the north.

The woman smiled and said something in English, stroking Laura's hair. Then she laid a hand at the base of her throat and said two words I had heard before, "Lily Hertert."

I hurried to the kitchen and brought back the bag of sugar, pointing to it and to her as I said, *"Tak! Tusind tak!"* She seemed to understand that I was thanking her and asking her to sit down on a packing case chair while I went to put the coffee on.

Fager was the word for Lily Hertert. She was indeed fair with cool, pale hair worn in a high puff and large, gray eyes that glowed with intelligence. She was tall and full-breasted with long, white fingers that showed no evidence of hard work.

Our first meeting turned into a language lesson that began as a game for Laura, and when Peter came home that night, I proudly thumped the table and said, *"Bord* is ta-ble!" Then I showed off with the easy ones like coffee and *kaffe*, doctor and *doktor*, and daughter and *datter*.

I was eager to know more about Lily than she could tell me, and Peter informed me that her husband was a banker, that her family had come to Massachusetts from England in the early years of the century, and that Lily herself had been a school mistress in a private academy in the east.

"She is beautiful, Far," Laura said, scratching at the green-brown film on her arms.

"She is too forward," Peter said, "and she interferes in her husband's business. If Lily does not like a person, she forbids John Hertert to lend him money."

"You have learned a great deal about her in a few months," I said, banging a bowl of bread and milk on the table before him.

"I have learned a great deal about everybody who lives in Harlan. Our livelihood depends on my knowing whether women like Lily Hertert prefer voile or dimity, whether Andrew Nicolai at the livery stable wants chewing tobacco or snuff, whether Clara Oxler, the dressmaker, is using wide ribbon or narrow this season. Amalie, do sit down and join us at our banquet!"

The banqueting on bread and milk went on for days and seemed to bring us no relief. Each morning we were marked with new welts.

The flour mill across the street began to hum before the sun came up, and though Peter and Laura slept through its demented singing, I would wake, put on a wrapper, and walk out into the dew. In the predawn half-light, I would scratch my burning skin and strain to see the wild flowers in the prairie that stretched eastward from our chicken house.

I did not know the American names of familiar flowers, and there were many that I never had seen. I loved the shooting star, a diving bird with purple petals for wings. Ironweed blossoms like rose lace, the pale pink saucers of the wild rose, and the joyous yellow of daisy fleabane and wild mustard vied for my next preference. If I squinted my eyes, the mantle of Queen Anne's lace could look like snow on the prairie.

When the rooster crowed, I walked back toward the house, and it was then that I noticed a dark, moving line on the wooden fence that ran from the chicken house to our back porch. An army of tiny bugs was returning from a sneak attack on the Jorgens!

I woke Peter, and as soon as the marching vermin had regained the chicken house, he tore down the section of the fence nearest the house, depriving them of their highway. Then he crated up the chickens for return to the farm where he had bought them and set fire to the chicken house.

Doctor Gus found us in the backyard watching the blaze. I didn't want Peter to tell him what we had discovered, because I thought he would be humiliated by his mistaken diagnosis, but Peter told me that Americans did not worry about feeling small. He was right. Doctor Gus laughed about the "crawling hives" and joined us for breakfast, letting Laura sit on his knee and play with his watch chain.

Americans were strange people, I thought, imagining how these circumstances would offend Herr Doctor Lervad of Ribe. I also wondered if a doctor who couldn't tell bug bites from hives could deliver a baby properly, but doubt could not survive in the presence of Doctor Gus. The very air around him was charged with health and confidence, and his honesty in admitting a mistake was part of it.

A few weeks later, the birth pains began, and I sent Peter for the doctor. Then Peter took Laura for a long walk, leaving me with no interpreter.

Doctor Gus and I talked, each in our own language, and somehow we seemed to understand each other. I knew what he meant when he said, "Go ahead and yell a little," but I had no intention of taking him at his word.

When he laid my American child in my arms, I struggled to remember his exact words so I could ask Peter what they meant.

"A daughter—a very fine specimen! Good girl!"

We named her Valborg. Laura put her doll in the cradle as a gift for her sister. Lily Hertert brought an armful of Austrian copper roses and a lace bonnet. Peter was proud, though I knew he had hoped for a son.

Tiny as Valborg was, her presence made the three-room house seem intolerably small. Peter went looking for a larger one with great enthusiasm. He would come home and describe the places he had looked at, rejecting some for crude carpentry and others for the arrangement of the rooms.

"But can we afford what you want, Peter?"

"Don't worry, I have a loan from John Hertert's bank."

At last we found a house that combined a sense of Danish snugness with a rambling American roominess. It was white frame with long porches, set on one of three lots surrounded by a picket fence on Willow street. It was in the best part of town, away from the flour mill.

Again Peter spent more money than I considered wise on furniture, but I loved the settee of curvy Victorian design and the reddish cherry wood of the marble-topped tables and chests. The lady chair he bought for me was as graceful as a well-formed woman, and it made the straight cane-seated chairs I had from my mother's house look stern and austere.

Being the mistress of this house was a delight. Its upkeep and the care of Valborg left me little time to study the language, which Laura was learning quickly, as children will. If she grew away from me thereby, I didn't notice, for I had Valborg, who loved my Danish lullabies.

I studied the town, however, as if it were a geography lesson, questioning Peter until he wondered at my obsession with the subject.

The Beehive was one of eight general merchandise stores that competed briskly for the trade in dry goods, household supplies, and notions. There were four pharmacies; three banks; three grocery and crockery stores; two bakers; three meat markets; two clothing, hat and cap stores; three hardware stores; two furniture and undertaking establishments; two jewelers; six restaurants; four boot and shoemakers; five saloons; three hotels; and three merchant tailors—all doing business on a town square constructed in the Spanish manner. A frame courthouse was the jewel of this setting, but there was talk of building a new one of stone.

Other businesses were close by on streets that extended from the sides of the Square: a fence factory; two butter and egg dealers; a housemover; a telephone exchange; three newspapers; three dressmakers; three harness-makers; two brickyards; three lumberyards; a book and news store; four coal dealers; four blacksmiths; five paint shops; and four farm implement dealers.

The grist mills were farther from the center of town, one operated by steam and the other by water. The steam-driven mill was the one across the street from our first home.

Tucked into the second-story rooms of the buildings on the Square were eighteen lawyers, two brokers, five land and loan agents, five grain dealers, two photographers, eleven doctors, two surveyors, and a dentist.

Discreet signs in the lace-curtained windows of modest houses advertised piano lessons and instruction in fine stitchery.

Peter's store, the Beehive, was on the ground floor of the

brick opera house, and he credited Edward Parmeter with the shrewd idea of taking this expensive space because of its advertising value.

"Every time people attend an opera house performance, they must pass our windows," he said, "they form the Beehive habit without realizing it. That Edward is a wonder!"

I could not share Peter's enthusiasm for Parmeter. I met him at last when Valborg was about two months old, and I didn't like the way he looked at me. He had the coldest blue eyes I ever saw, and yet they burned right through my new dress of purple-sprigged voile. He managed to brush against my hand or arm when there was no need. He moved, it seemed to me, with a sinister grace that I despised and yet admired. My reaction to Parmeter was similar to the way I felt about a beautifully marked snake. When I saw one, I wanted to run, and yet I longed to stay and stare at it.

I was subjected to this conflict daily, for Peter liked to have me stop by at the Beehive every afternoon. It pleased him to have me dress up, adorn our daughters with ribbons and ruffles, and stroll to the Square pushing Valborg in her perambulator. He had just discovered the paintings of Renoir, and he saw us as a living composition after the French artist.

Our route was a ritual: up Eighth street to Baldwin, then along the west and north sides of the Square to the Beehive, where Peter would be waiting for us. The store was pleasantly dim after the glare of the streets, and Peter would touch my elbow to guide me until my eyes grew accustomed to the changed light. In those moments of semi-blindness, I could better appreciate the medicinal smell of bolts of cloth, the pungent odor of snuff, and the aroma of the coffee that was brewing on a tiny, black iron stove in the back room.

I always brought almond cakes or *smäkager* from home, and Edward Parmeter would join us for afternoon coffee while

Laura played hide-and-seek with Cora, the middle-aged clerk, who was very kind to children when she was not busy. Edward had presented me with a cup painted with valley lilies for these occasions, and he stared at me until I could scarcely drink from it. I grew hot with confusion and didn't know where to look.

Speaking to Peter in Danish, I said, "He makes me uncomfortable. I don't think I will come tomorrow."

"Don't be foolish, Amalie, he is just admiring you, as I want everyone to do. You *must* come. It makes me proud!"

And so I continued my visits to the Beehive except on days when the damp summer heat pressed down like an anvil on my chest. I was not accustomed to such extreme weather, for the warmth of the Danish summer is soft as a caress. When the heat waves danced up from the brick streets, I kept the children inside and closed doors and windows against the season's hot breath.

Laura was frightened by the violent summer storms with their thunder and lightening. I told her that Thor and Odin had discovered America too, and that here there was more room for them to stalk about and get noisy.

162

17

Valborg was not baptized until she was old enough to walk, be-cause Peter thought we should join an American church. He had visited the Methodists, Congregationalists, Baptists, Christians, and Latter Day Saints to make a choice and had established himself in the Christian Church before Laura and I came.

I did not become a member, but I went with him to the white frame building with its delicate belfry of carved wood on Sundays. The Service was almost meaningless to me, but I sat with Peter and the girls in a hard varnished pew to partake of the Lord's Supper, which was served weekly, and I tried to lis-ten to the urgent preaching. The ecclesiastical tone transcends language, and I knew that I was in church, but I received none of the comfort offered by the Lutheran liturgy in my own lan-guage.

Pastor P.S. Sorensen, a Dane who lived in Harlan and served a Danish Lutheran church in Bowman's Grove, came to call on us. He urged us to drive to the little settlement in the grove to worship with our fellow Danes on the Sabbath, and I wanted to so much, but I could not persuade Peter to change.

In the meantime, Valborg remained unbaptized, for the Christian Church members did not take this step until the age of discretion. I would not have worried if it had not been for Dagmar Jensen. She and Gunnar were staunch members of Bowman's Grove Lutheran congregation, and she urged me to have Pastor Sorensen baptize Valborg immediately.

"This is a serious matter among us," she said, "especially when someone in the family is a Baptist. Rigmor Mathiesen is a Baptist, and she and her husband are pulling their poor baby in two! Hans insists on Lutheran baptism now, but Rigmor says if he goes through with it, she will bring the child up in a way to make his baptism ineffective."

"Why doesn't she let Hans have his way? Then she can have the child re-baptized at the time she thinks is right."

Dagmar gasped, "One does not trifle with such things! I could not bear to think that any child of mine was unbaptized!"

I spoke to Peter about it that evening, and he made light of my concern.

"Many boxes are built to hold God, Amalie, and our box is just as good as the Lutheran box. Valborg can be baptized in due time."

He bounced the baby on his knee while the properly baptized Laura tried to braid one side of his full moustache.

I could not believe that Peter was right about the baptism, and I brooded about it while he told me of a dance at Long's Hall to be followed by a midnight supper at the Harlan House. Edward Parmeter had invited Gertrude Wyland, and we were to go with them.

"The music is to be played by the Northwestern Quadrille Band of Clinton. Just think, Amalie, they are coming all the way across the state to play for us! It is as if a band from Ribe were to play at Grenen! Amalie, do you realize that we have never danced together in America?"

How could he speak of dancing when Valborg's soul might be in jeopardy? I would have her baptized in secret as soon as I could arrange it.

"You shall have a new dress," he was saying; "go to Mrs. Oxler tomorrow and have her measure you. Of all the dressmakers who come into the store, I think she is the best. I asked Edward, and he thought so too."

"I scarcely need Mr. Parmeter's help in choosing a dressmaker!" I said haughtily, and Peter laughed.

The new dress, which was cream silk and as beautiful as any gown from Paris, was my pretext for being away from home without questions. Lily Hertert took care of the girls when I went for fittings, leaving me free to stop by the parsonage on the way home to arrange Valborg's baptism with Pastor Sorensen. When I needed Valborg for the actual event, I told Lily that I promised Mrs. Oxler I would bring the baby along the next time. I did take her with me for an unnecessary consultation on the width of the lace for the neck of the gown, then hurried to the parsonage, where Dagmar and Gunnar were waiting.

"Thank God!" Dagmar said. "I was afraid you had changed your mind!"

"Let's hurry," I said nervously.

Gunnar produced a pair of white boots he had made for Valborg as a baptismal gift, and I could see that they were too small, but I thanked him and tucked them into my reticule.

Pastor Sorensen was wearing his Danish clerical ruff, and the dear, familiar sight filled my eyes with tears. The baptismal font from the Bowman's Grove church stood in the parlor, where we assembled to hear the time-honored words spoken over our infants for generations without number.

Valborg Kathrine was a wriggling armful for the pastor, and

as he carried the palmful of baptismal water to her head, she arched her back and made him spill almost all of it on the rug. I wondered what this could mean, reverting to the spell of signs and portents for the first time since coming to America.

The American superstitions I had heard about were nonmystical, dealing with the removal of warts, the successful canning of green beans, and good fortune in courting. These were of little interest to me, for I had no warts, knew how to can beans without failure, and had Peter.

Lily invited me for afternoon tea, and while I was bursting to talk about Valborg's baptism, it was nothing I could discuss with her. Lily was a Unitarian, something close to the Danish Deists, I gathered, and she considered traditional Protestant views to be unenlightened.

A few others in Harlan shared her ideas, and they met in each other's homes to read Emerson and Thoreau. Lily could give me a vague understanding of these matters because she spoke slowly to me, finding recognizable substitutes for the words that gave me trouble. She also spoke German, which I had heard in Ribe and understood better than I would admit. My prejudice against the Prussians was of such long standing that I resisted their tongue.

"It is the language of Goethe and Schiller," Lily told me, "so it can't be all bad. What do you read, Amalie?"

"Swedenborg—"

"That's barbarous! Let me give you something better." She rose from the tea table, moving like a willow tree taking up its roots to glide to a new growing spot, and I followed her to the library.

This room contained the largest private collection of books I had seen. Shelves reached to the ceiling, and the top volumes could be reached by climbing a tall ladder that moved on tracks. The printed titles told me nothing, for the little English I had was oral, but I was struck by the beauty of the books themselves: creamy calf, maroon leather, green moire, whorled designs like mottled marble.

Lily trailed a white finger along a shelf until it flew like the forked stick of a dowser to a deep red volume.

"Montaigne! The very thing! You cannot read in this book for very long without having your mind filled and lined. Montaigne is the French Horace, and while this is a translation, the vigor still comes through."

I breathed in her lavender scent as she held the book for me and pointed with a schoolmistressy finger. I was certain that I would disappoint her, for the printed words were no more than bird tracks to me, but I took the book and promised to try to get something from it.

We were home long before Peter, for he had stayed at the store after closing to work on the books, and with our *middag* ready to serve the moment he appeared, I had time to sit down with Montaigne. I could not read one word.

Peter found me scowling over the incomprehensible pages and took the book from me, translating into Danish as he read, "I never knew father, how crooked and deformed soever his son were, that would either altogether cast him off, or not acknowledge him for his own."

Montaigne didn't know *my* father, I thought, then asked Peter to point out each word individually for me. In this way I would slowly conquer the essays of Montaigne and learn archaic English spellings that would have to be unlearned.

Thinking about the dance at Long's Hall upset me. My dress was ready, but I was not.

What would I say to people in my sparse, broken English? Peter insisted that I said "good evening" like a born American, and that, plus a smile, would suffice.

What if somebody asked me to dance? I knew no American steps. Peter said the waltz was international.

The day before the dance, Peter took me to the studio of Dammand, the photographer. Dammand was a big, untidy man who emerged from the black tent over his camera like some swamp monster, and his hands were rough in adjusting the clamps that held our heads while he performed his mysterious motions.

Peter sat on a piano stool, and I stood behind him resting one hand on his shoulder. The head clamp bit through my hair, and I tried to offset the pressure by pushing down on Peter.

Dammand held up a pan on a stick and somehow set off a Mephistophelian explosion that filled the room with smoke. He fixed us forever in attitudes we never had assumed before and never would repeat. We were the nouveau Americans: Peter looking pugnacious in his high-buttoned vest and looped cravat and Amalie struck by lofty thoughts in her cream silk ball gown.

We presented a livelier picture when we set out for Long's Hall in the same garb. We had toasted each other in *snaps* before Cora came to stay with the children, and I was sucking a clove to conceal the cause of my gaiety. As far as I knew, all the ladies of Harlan were temperance, except Lily, who clung to her pre-dinner sherry as a mark of civilization.

First we called for Edward Parmeter at the Harlan House, where he maintained his bachelor quarters. He was splendid in a dove-gray coat, and a discreetly delicate barbershop aroma moved with him into the carriage.

"You should always look as you do tonight," he said.

Peter explained that we had been photographed to insure the permanence of our elegance.

"Photographs are cold," Edward said, looking straight at

me; "you are not."

"Indeed we are not!" Peter laughed, "We are primed with akvavit!"

"I had a little something myself," Edward admitted; "the fair Gertrude is far more northern than you Scandinavians, and I wanted to fortify myself against the chill."

Gertrude Wyland was the only child of Stacher Wyland, who platted Harlan. She lived with her father in a big house in a park-like enclosure fenced with ornamental ironwork with the name "Idylwyld" lettered in an arch above the gate. A bulkily draped marble Diana perpetually drew her bow at a metal stag across the walk that led to the long, deep front porch.

Gertrude was thin as a bed slat, and she wore tiny, oval glasses with thin gold rims. She towered above Edward's considerable height.

She said "Good evening," then nothing more until the horses were tied to the long rail in front of the hall. "I feel a blinding headache coming on!"

"Amalie will take you to the ladies' parlor," Peter offered, "or perhaps you'd rather be taken home?"

Edward watched her with a tiny, ironic smile as she declined both suggestions and headed for the ladies' parlor alone. "Peter, you'll have to share your wife tonight!"

Thus, I arrived with two escorts. The main hall was crowded with dancing couples, and the straight-backed chairs along the walls were occupied by the old, the shy, and the unwanted. I recognized scarcely anyone, and no one at all was there from our church.

The Northwestern Quadrille Band was in full evening dress with red sashes like those of stage nobility. The trumpet players blew so lustily that the wind from their horns swayed the red and white bunting draped around the platform.

Edward asked me to dance the schottische, but I declined,

saying I must dance with my husband first. I tapped my foot under the cover of my wide skirt until Peter claimed me for the waltz.

After this dance, I would have to find some other excuse for Edward, but now I closed my eyes as we glided and dipped, grew pleasantly dizzy, and imagined myself back at Fairwoods, where we had danced to celebrate the birthday of Dich and Dines. I did not know that the other dancers had cleared the floor for us until I opened my eyes at the sound of loud clapping.

"Beautiful! Simply beautiful!" Lily Hertert was saying.

Peter was pleased by the applause, but it abashed me, and I found a chair, where I sat fanning myself furiously.

From then on, one man after another asked me to dance. Ed Cane, the lawyer; Roger Lucas, editor of the Harlan Hub; and Francis Richardson, the strange man who walked about the county lending money. I declined all invitations until Doctor Gus stood before me and bowed. The faint smell of ether was still upon him and his tangled curls were as wild as ever. He danced clumsily, but I was comfortable with him.

I told him about Gertrude Wyland's indisposition and suggested that he go to her.

"She doesn't need my kind of doctoring. She ought to leave this town and go where an honest man might take her for what she is."

Then Edward Parmeter was tapping Doctor Gus's shoulder. In Edward's arms, I couldn't seem to manage my feet. I was humiliated when I stepped on his pumps, and I longed for the music to end, but he seemed to take pleasure in my confusion.

The midnight supper that waited for us at the Harlan House was elaborate beyond my expectations. Within minutes the hungry dancers had reduced the perfectly browned chicken, the great joints of ham, the mountains of mashed potatoes, and the heaping dishes of piccalilli to a messy rubble. Gertrude Wyland, who had recovered from her headache with the last strains of the dance music, ate heartily, and the members of the Northwestern Quadrille Band fell upon the food as if they hadn't eaten for days.

The sky was pinkish-gray when we drove home, but Peter and I were wide awake. We made love under the weeping willow near the back fence before creeping into the quiet house.

Some days passed before we learned that we had sinned. The pastor called to bring it to our attention. As he kindly put it, "You are foreigners and can't be expected to know these things."

Dancing was wicked; a snare of the Devil. Drinking spirits was not to be tolerated. He did not mention al fresco lovemaking, which gave us our beautiful Else.

18

Else was such a perfect baby. When we knew I was pregnant again, we expected another child like her, but Kamille was scrawny and colicky.

"We must get back to the land and give her a chance to grow!" Peter said.

"But we can see plowed fields from our front porch!"

"It's not the same," he said, and before the day was out, he had bought a farm where I could spend the summer with our four daughters. He hired a young immigrant named Berg Landsman to till the land and take care of the pigs and cattle.

Kamille outgrew her colic after our first two weeks in the country and Peter was jubilant. He came to the farm on Saturday nights and drove back to Harlan on Monday mornings. While he was with us, I cooked lavishly and saw to it that the Jorgen females were dressed prettily, but the rest of the time we went barefoot and took many of our simple meals under the trees near the banks of the Nishnabotna. The Indian name meant "canoe-building river." The tributary on our land was wider than the Odense river but just as winding, and when the water was high, it flowed chocolate-brown with its load of rich Iowa soil.

Except for Horst Reimer to the east of us, the neighboring farmers were Yankees. They made fun of Berg, who could speak no English, I watched them engage him at the property lines, making sport of him in words he couldn't understand, though he gathered their meaning. His neck burned dull red, but he said nothing. I wanted to rescue him but knew this would humiliate him more.

"Don't mind them, Berg!"

"I take better care of the land than they do," he said brooding.

"Of course you do, and you'll have your own land someday."

Percy McConnell, the big, loud hired man from the Reimer place, took particular pleasure in tormenting Berg. I often saw McConnell lurking in the trees near the river, absolutely bloated with mischief as he watched Berg trudging behind the plow. McConnell would imitate the blood-chilling cry of the prairie wolf to perfection, laughing with idiotic glee when Berg's head snapped up in alarm.

One day when Berg was working with the long-handled scythe in a near field, I saw him stop mid-swing and slowly lower the blade. He knelt, holding out one hand in the silent coaxing of some creature I could not see. Suddenly McConnell yelled from the trees. Berg fell back on his heels, covering his eyes with his forearm and choking violently. The wind carried a fierce acrid odor to the spot where I stood, and as I ran toward Berg, the smell grew stronger and more repulsive.

McConnell came out of the trees in a grotesque, thigh-slapping dance, gasping with laughter.

"Nice kitty, sweet tabby!" he whooped, "You dumb Dane, don't you know a skunk when you see one?"

I followed the line of his pointing finger and saw a black, glossy animal with a bushy tail and a broad white stripe down its back streaking toward the trees.

Picking up the scythe that Berg had dropped, I advanced on McConnell threateningly. "Get out! Don't come back here!"

He laughed nastily, jerking a thumb at Berg. "He your sweety? He won't smell so sweet tonight!"

If Laura and Valborg hadn't been running toward us pulling Else and the baby in a little wagon, I'm sure I would have buried the scythe blade in whatever part of McConnell I could reach, but I saw them coming and dropped my weapon.

"Phew, Mama, what smells?" Laura asked.

The sight of the little girls with the sun glinting in hair that was every shade of ripening wheat had an effect on McConnell.

"Well, ain't they pretty?" he said, clasping his hands behind his back, "Better get'em out of this skunk stink."

As we retreated from the field, the odor went with us. I sent Berg down to the river with a bar of lye soap and pumped and carried two washtubs of water from the upper well to bathe the rest of us. The clothes Berg had worn were so odorous that no amount of boiling and scrubbing could remove the awful smell. In the end, I burned them, which hurt my frugal nature and Berg's. Later a neighbor told me I could have buried them and let the ground draw out the scent. He said too that the skunk would not have used this rank weapon if it hadn't been frightened; knowledge that added fuel to our burning grudge against Percy McConnell.

A Dane does not anger quickly, but his rage can be awesome after a long smouldering. McConnell should not have tried to drop a garter snake into Berg's burlap-covered water jug. It happened on a Monday morning just after Peter drove back to town, and Berg gave McConnell a terrible beating.

"Oh Berg," I said, looking down at the unconscious hired man, "that was not Christian!"

He wiped his mouth with the back of his hand, pushed a shock of white-blond hair from his eyes, and quoted Grundtvig, "First be a man, then a Christian! What shall I do with him?"

We had a triple box lumber wagon in the shed, and I told Berg to hitch the plow horse to it.

"I'll take him to the Reimers and explain."

McConnell was beginning to stir and groan, so I didn't take the time to comb my hair and put on a fresh dress. I must have been a wild sight as I clattered into the Reimers' rutted lane with the cursing hired man rising on one elbow in the wagon behind me.

Horst Reimer came from his orchard with a pruning hook in his hand, and I haltingly explained, "That one tormented Berg, and it was too much for him."

Reimer shifted a wad of chewing tobacco to his other cheek, hefting the hook reflectively. He walked to the side of the wagon to inspect McConnell.

"Your man is stout!" he said.

"I'm sorry, but yours deserved it!"

"I've no doubt that Percy was spoilin' for it. He's a bad one, but I can't get nobody else. Percy, crawl out of that wagon and get to work!"

"He can't!" I protested. Much as I despised McConnell, I thought it was cruel to expect anything from him for at least a week.

"Any time he loses, I'll have to charge it to you, Missus. I got crops to get in."

"My husband will pay!" I said grandly. "Please take your man out of my wagon and let him rest until he is well."

"Bertha!" Reimer bellowed, and his wife scuttled out of the house to help with the invalid. Her face was tired and meager in its narrow frame of tightly pulled hair, and her look was hostile, for I had added to her burdens.

"I'm very sorry," I told her in German, and she was softened momentarily by the sound of her native tongue. These were the last words to be spoken between the Jorgens and the Reimers.

Berg Landsman had spent two winters at a Folk High School in South Jutland, and when the evening chores were finished, he would sit at the kitchen table reading. Laura, who was very proud of the advances she had made in her McGuffey Readers, sat opposite with a storybook Peter had ordered from a salesman who came to the Beehive.

"Why does Berg read, Mama?" she asked, "He is too old for school."

I told her what Christen Kold, one of the first practitioners of N.F.S. Grundtvig's educational theories, had often said: "My aim is to wind up my students so they will keep going for life." I always remembered this because it reminded me of Far's dozens of ticking timepieces.

The evenings of reading seemed long to me, for the only book I had was Hop-Caroline's Bible. I had left everything else in town. Berg and Laura sat motionless in the golden ocher light from the kerosene lamp, unmindful of the moths that fluttered to the glass chimney, while I moved about restlessly. I brought coffee and *klejner* or *jødekager* to the table or strolled to the porch to listen to the crickets and the distant hooting of owls in the trees near the river.

I worried vaguely about the owls preying on the Black Minorcas in the henhouse and wondered why the setting of the sun did so little to relieve the oppressive heat of the summer day. I thought how the next day would be the same as this one and wondered what Peter was doing to while away a summer night in Harlan. I walked into the tiny bedroom the three older girls shared and pulled the sheets up over the sweaty, jumbled limbs of Valborg and Else, then looked in on Kamille, who breathed with alarming catches and gurgles when she slept. Finally I left the house and opened the slanting doors of the root cellar to stand in the cooling breath of dank air that rushed upward. When something cold slithered across my bare foot, I let out a shriek that brought Berg on the run.

The snake was far away before he let me go, and I think he was as glad for the darkness as I was. I turned to go back to the house without saying a word to him, and he did not come for some time. When he did, he gathered up his books with great finality, and we both knew we never would be easy with each other again. After blood has spoken to blood, simple friendship is impossible.

When Peter came that Friday evening, I clung to him so fiercely that he laughed, "Edward is quite right. Absence *does* make the heart grow fonder!"

"Edward is a fine one to speak of hearts!" I snapped, "He has none!"

"Come now, he's been seeing Lily's niece from Boston and showing every sign of being in love."

"Is she rich?"

"Only in natural endowments. She has just finished Normal School and will go to Colorado to teach in the fall."

This piece of news upset me beyond reason, and I was angry with myself for the way I felt until I convinced myself that I was concerned for Lily's relative. Lily would drive out for a visit soon, and I would warn her about Edward.

How glad I was for the visit of Emmanuel Jul! Jul was a walking peddler who stocked books, as well as an array of laces, handkerchiefs, needles, and notions.

The girls saw him coming a long way off and mistook his bulky, canvas knapsack for a hump on his back. Their excitement rose as he came closer, each plodding footstep raising a puff of dust.

I met him at the door with a dipperful of cold well water. He took it gratefully, but when I responded to his thanks in Danish, disappointment showed in his sun-bleached blue eyes.

"Ah, Fru Jorgen, wouldn't you like to practice your English with me?"

"No, please, I love to hear my own tongue."

As he emptied his knapsack on the kitchen table, I went through the books eagerly, finding Grundtvig's works, Otto Møller's theological treatises, and Frederick Nielsen's Church History.

Jul must have caught my quickly suppressed sigh, for he said, "These are fine books! Uplifting books! As for cheap, sentimental fiction, my legs will not carry such dung and trash!"

I noticed an impediment in his speech, which he explained.

Jul had gone to a Folk High School, but the eloquence there only emphasized his defect, and he left to study on his own. He had been in America six years longer than we had, and somehow the new language mitigated his problem. In the new land there were many kinds of speech, and people didn't seem to notice his difficulty.

He spoke of Kimballton, the settlement that might have been a bit of Denmark transplanted, laughing and slapping his knee as he told of the Italian shoemaker who had settled there, learned enough Danish to carry on his trade, then discovered that he had learned not English, but a second foreign language.

I made coffee for Emmanuel Jul, enjoying his cheerful chatter and loving him because he was the embodiment of my fairy tale father. We discovered many mutual friends, and he told me that Dagmar Jensen was expecting another baby.

"I love to bring good news," he said, marking wet crescents in his dusty face with the rim of one of the deep crockery cups I used on the farm.

"Don't you get tired of walking?"

"When I do, I catch a ride. If I'm headed east, I can tend cattle on a stock train for my fare. Steers are wonderfully warm traveling companions in the winter! Now, what about the books? Surely there is something you would enjoy!"

Jul's books reminded me of the contents of Pastor Madsen's shelves in Ausig, and I couldn't bring myself to buy any of them, but I did choose six handkerchiefs and a special pleating iron that I could have had cheaper from the Beehive.

Somehow I must pay him for coming, for his short visit had broken the dull sameness of my days and freshened everything like an east wind on a sultry day.

Remembering what had happened to my father, I worried about his walking the roads in every kind of weather.

"Don't you ever want to settle down and stay in one place?"

The tiny, sun-shrunk pupils of his eyes were fixed on the small square of horizon we could see through the open door as he answered.

"Sometimes I try, but never for long. There is always a hill that hides the very thing I must see, and I must climb to look. Then what do I see? 'I will lift mine eyes unto the hills—.' I wanted to be a pastor, you know, but how could a tongue like mine preach? Once I saw this written on a tombstone: 'I believed, therefore I spoke.' Isn't that beautiful? I would give much to have such words above my last resting place, but it can't be." He sighed deeply, then smiled, unwilling to depart on such a wistful note. "I'll come your way again. Is there something special I can bring you?"

"Yes, there is. All the good, human stories about people aren't dung and trash. Bring me a book as true as life."

"If there is one I am willing to carry, I will bring it to you," he promised.

When I learned that I was pregnant for the seventh time, I resigned myself to producing another daughter.

As soon as Peter came out from town, I told him, and he held me close there in the farmyard.

"Peter, will you mind terribly if it's a girl again?"

"Not if you do as well as before," he said, but I knew he was thinking of our little boys, gone these many years.

I was brought to bed on a bright April day, and the labor was brief. So brief that Doctor Gus was still scrubbing at our kitchen sink when I called out, "Hurry, or I won't need you!"

Dazed by the pain, I didn't trust my ears when they heard, "This young fellow was in an all-fired hurry to get here!"

Peter, who was waiting outside the door, heard it too, and he shouted jubilantly, "A boy!"

"Oh, let me see him!" I begged, but I had to wait while the practical nurse cleaned the baby. Then Peter and I yearned over him, afraid to believe in our luck.

He was fair and well-formed. Looking at him, I felt a fleeting curiosity about the girl who would someday draw him to her with a cherry-red ribbon.

"What shall we name him?" Peter asked, for we hadn't thought about names for a boy.

"Anything but Karsten!"

We talked and thought and talked again until we agreed on Stig. Stig Jorgen.

"Now my name will go on," Peter said with deep emotion. "Life has given me everything!"

On the farm, where life was completely casual, I could devote most of my attention to my baby, and Stig flourished. His sisters treated him like a big doll, showing no signs of jealousy.

"Next year he'll be big enough to ride!" Peter said, and I laughed.

Stig tried to make that prophecy come true the following summer. He was making a fierce attempt to clamber up the foreleg of Ophelia, the patient, old dray horse, when I snatched him to safety.

"He's a real boy!" Peter said proudly when I told him about it.

I said nothing, knowing this was the first of many incidents that would make my heart thunder with motherly fear for Stig.

We always left the farm the last week in August to get the children ready for school, but it was not goodbye, for we saw our farm neighbors again at the fall husking contests.

The competition ran from daylight to sunset, and many of the spectators came and went during the long hours, but some people made a day of it, bringing baskets of food to eat in their carriages where they sat wrapped in buffalo robes while the contestants doggedly stripped the contest field.

When we got cold, we jumped down and stood around a big bonfire that blazed all day, and Peter would warm bricks in it for our feet.

I came out just for the afternoon on the day that George Slaughter cribbed the last of 685 bushels of corn in a six-day marathon to take the championship. His hands were raw under the shredded gloves that dropped to the ground as the leather straps on his wrists were unbuckled.

Sitting in our carriage in my russet velvet suit with its braid-trimmed cape, I flexed my hands in their thin chamois gloves, incapable of imagining that someday my wrists would be strapped with leather for the same task. At that time Stig was just learning to walk, and my heaviest exertion consisted of chasing after him until the bigger girls came home from school to spell me.

Laura was thirteen now, and she had the sweet gravity of a young married woman. Strangers always took her to be older than she was. She adored Stig, as we all did, and she was stern with him for his own good.

She did not go to the corn husking marathon with us, for it was a school day, and I wished for her as Stig grew increasingly rambunctious.

After we congratulated the exhausted George Slaughter, we walked back to our carriage to drive home. Peter was carrying Stig on his shoulders, and neither of us saw the corncobs in both fat fists until they beat a tattoo on Peter's hat, ramming it down over his eyes. He stumbled and nearly fell, but he laughed, swinging Stig downward into his arms and telling him to drop the cobs.

Stig held on tightly, and when Peter forced his fingers open, he strained toward the fallen treasures and cried with rage. Peter struck his well-padded bottom with an open palm, which increased the howls, and young as he was, Stig carried a grudge against his father for days.

It was funny and pathetic, and I tried to stay out of the matter, but I must confess to showing Stig a furtive tenderness that undermined his father's authority. I had lost two sons and was foolish about the third. Even Laura would have known better.

184

19

Not far from Harlan, though it seemed far by horse and buggy measurement, was Elk Horn, a Danish settlement that boasted a Folk High School. The original building, raised by farmers in the surrounding country in 1878, burned in 1886, but it was speedily rebuilt to maintain a core of Danish culture far from the homeland.

On September 8, the birthday of N.F.S. Grundtvig, we took Laura and Valborg with us to the special celebration at the school.

The countryside southeast of Harlan was the Danish landscape raised to a higher power. The hills were taller and the valleys were deeper. Instead of the sheltering intimacy of near horizons, there was unbounded distance, and the Danish sense of sky cupping the land like a protective hand gave way to clear, bright infinity. Still, Iowa was America's closest approximation of our native land. Except for the difference in scope, we might have been on the Jutland moorlands.

We crossed several miles of blackened stubble left by a prairie fire that brought back memories of the charred remains of the store in Ribe.

Not far from our destination, Peter stopped the horses to let us examine two heaps of elk horns; exotic cairns to our eyes.

"Don't get down," he warned, "there are rattlesnakes. The students are brought out to look at these horns and taken twenty miles to the south to see the ruts of the old Mormon Trail."

"What's the Mormon Trail, Papa?" Valborg asked, one foot already dangling from the buggy in an impish prelude to disobedience.

Peter flicked her little white stocking with the buggy whip, his hand punishing while his voice pleasantly informed her about the Mormons walking through Iowa behind their handcarts after they were hounded from the beautiful city they had built in the swampy wilderness at Nauvoo, Illinois.

"Your Uncle Ib is a Mormon," he finished.

I wondered if Ib would have kept the faith behind a handcart. He had come to the Mormons later, after they had reached their promised land, but he might have lasted through the impossibly difficult trek. We were stubborn people.

We arrived at the Elk Horn school just at sunset, and supper was waiting in the lecture hall, the only room big enough to accommodate the crowd. There was pork and red cabbage, *frikadeller,* soup with fishballs made from Nishnabotna carp, home-cured ham, pumpernickel, and pastries that flaked and melted before the teeth could touch them.

Smiling farm wives replenished the dishes on the long plank tables before they showed depletion. Peter filled his plate with sugar-fried potatoes three times, which made me blush because people would think I didn't feed him at home.

Dagmar Jensen had made me extremely sensitive about the opinions of my fellow Danes by intimating that I had "gone Yankee" and drifted away from my countrymen.

"That isn't true!" I would say, feeling secretly guilty about our American church, rare roast beef, and a houseful of Yankee furniture.

Here at Elk Horn I could wallow in Danishness: the faith, the food, the language, and the school brought back memories of Sandinge. Several young teachers fresh from Denmark made me homesick with their talk of Copenhagen and Roskilde.

I put Valborg in Laura's charge and set out to talk to as many of my compatriots as possible, leaving Peter to joke with the girl students, whose tongues were sharp, however countrified their manners.

An older man with a thick, brush-like moustache handed me a fresh cup of coffee and introduced himself as Emanuel Vestergaard, a member of the original staff.

"You have a little Denmark here, Herr Vestergaard," I said, "and it seems a happy place."

"You know the old saying, Fru Jorgen, 'Grundtvigdianere are good company,' but we have had some difficult times. In the winter of 1880-81, the snow was so deep that we could not haul coal from Atlantic, so we burned corn. It seemed a sinful waste, but we could not save the corn and let the students freeze to death. You cannot talk to the heart and the mind when the body is cold, can you?"

I agreed that one could not and inquired about the curriculum, which was much like Sandinge's, including Scandinavian history, mythology, literature, and church history. Then our talk turned back to the hardships of the earlier immigrants.

"In 1869 ten people moved into a ten-by-fifteen-foot dugout and lived there all winter," Herr Vestergaard said. "Can you imagine that in the Iowa winter with wolves howling all around?"

I shuddered and shook my head. "The ten-by-ten board shanties with the cooking stove outside must have been better than that!"

Herr Vestergaard laughed. "Come and meet Niels Smidt. He can tell you how it was with those!"

Smidt was a white-haired old man with the neck of a bull who had bought out Yankees in all directions until he owned several sections of land. He crushed my fingers between two horny palms in greeting and told me about the partitions of his first house on the prairie.

"Walls cost money, Fru Jorgen," he said, "so I took a piece of chalk and drew lines on the floor. This square for Bodil, that one for Hans, a smaller one for the twins, and the biggest for me and Pouline. The floor was dirt, so the lines were never scrubbed away, and in time we had real walls. Do you know something? Walls you can thump work no better than chalk lines!" He laughed until he fell into a fit of coughing and had to go outside.

I wandered back toward Peter, dodging the busy women who were clearing the tables. I caught a glimpse of the sweet curve of Laura's back as she bent to hear something Valborg was saying to her, and I saw the frankly avid appraisal in the male eyes that shared my view. It took me by surprise. Laura was nearly grown up, and I had let her grow as untended as the heather on the moor because she gave me no trouble. Where was the Danishness I meant to nourish in her? Something must be done about this! I caught Peter's arm, interrupting his talk with a young teacher from Copenhagen, and said, "Laura must come here next summer!"

"No, Amalie. We have taken a new country, and our children must spend their whole energy learning its ways. In fact, there is something I have been meaning to speak to you about—"

"What?" I asked with a sense of misgiving. Peter never postponed speaking to me about anything unless he was expecting resistance. Not that I ever failed to give in to him, but sometimes I planted my feet long enough to make him uncomfortable, and he liked to put off such impasses as long as he could.

"We have a long drive home, we can talk about it then."

"No, I want to hear it now!" I glanced up to see Laura turn haughtily from a boy who reminded me of Birch Sandahl.

"Well, all right. Edward tells me there is a young teacher at the Harlan House who is looking for more permanent quarters. He is a relative of Edward's, and I thought we might offer him a room in return for some tutoring—"

I envisioned some strange young man's greasy hair on the lace pillow shams of our spare bedroom and tightened my lips.

Catching my expression, Peter spoke to me harshly.

"Do you think I would invite some lout into my home? Victor Lytle is here on Edward's recommendation. He is a graduate of the College of William and Mary, a gentleman educated in the classics. He can take his meals elsewhere if you'd rather not have him at table. Now, what do you say?"

I couldn't answer just then because Valborg had overturned a tureen of rødgrød on her hair and dress. I took her across the field to the school president's house to clean her up, and when I brought her back damp and pink, I found I had missed half of the president's commemorative lecture on Grundtvig. However, I was just in time to see a brash farm lad trying to push a note into Laura's lap. Perhaps she *did* need the tutoring of a gentleman.

"All right, Peter," I said as we walked to our buggy under a sky turned milky by uncountable stars, "let him come."

Victor Lytle arrived in a carriage from the livery stable. He knocked, introduced himself in a soft, drawling voice that made me wonder whether he was speaking English, and asked where he might direct the ostler to put his things.

With Stig and Kamille hanging on my skirts, I led the way

to the spare room that was my pride. Did I dare to ask him not to permeate the heavy damask draperies with cigar smoke?

He forestalled the question by volunteering, "I am not a user of tobacco, ma'am."

The ostler staggered in with a bound trunk of fine quality and two polished cowhide bags that proclaimed a fastidious owner.

Lytle immediately opened the trunk and took out half a dozen well-worn books, which he set between bookends carved in the likenesses of Plato and Aristotle. I knew because their names were incised in the bases. The way he looked at the books and handled them suggested an intimacy that outsiders should turn their eyes from, and I did.

"Now ma'am, if you will acquaint me with the schedule of the household, I will try to be as little trouble to you as possible. I require very little attention—only a bit of quiet for my studies."

Stig was eyeing the young man in a fashion that boded very little quiet, and Kamille was ready to join in a noisy appropriation of a new playmate. Before I could speak, they surged forward and embraced his legs, Stig at the knee and Kamille a bit higher. Those impeccable, close-cut trousers bunched in their clutch, and I held my breath as Lytle's long-fingered hands descended, but when they rested lightly on two cotton-blond heads, I knew all was well. Victor Lytle knelt and scooped both children up in his arms, saying, "This makes it perfect. I've never lived in a house without young'uns—except at college, and I'm not sure that's living."

"Are you hungry?" I asked, though I hadn't meant to let him eat with us.

With his eager nod, he became part of our household. At *middag,* which we now called supper, I sat him down with a makeshift napkin ring, an extra wooden loop from the parlor curtains, and I could see that he was impressed by the betterment of the children's manners when their father was present.

Peter always asked a lengthy blessing on the food, and if any hand reached out while the "amen" still echoed, he drenched the offender with the contents of his water glass. Else got the bath this time and left the table in tears. If Lytle was shocked at this extraordinary means of discipline, he didn't show it. Keeping his brown eyes on his plate, he ate with a slow fastidiousness, and when Peter probed for his interests, he answered courteously, almost deprecatingly. Still, the banked fires of his enthusiasm glowed hotly enough to kindle interest in Laura's gray-green eyes.

"I cannot pretend to understand the principles of business as you so admirably do, Mr. Jorgen," he said, "and I am afraid that my readings in Greek and Latin have little commercial value."

"Value attaches to that which gives pleasure," Peter said, "or so we thought in the Old Country. Perhaps things are different here."

"May I speak, Papa?" Laura asked shyly.

Peter nodded abruptly, brusque, as he often was when his feeling for his eldest daughter came too near the surface.

She spoke so softly that Victor Lytle had to lean forward to catch her words. I still can see the gaslight drawing a gleam from her chestnut hair and the white, blue-veined arc of her neck as she raised her chin and said, "To know is the most wonderful thing in the world!"

"To know what, Laura?" I asked, wanting to ground her, wanting to obscure Victor Lytle's recognition of her radiance in that moment. I knew the pitfalls of intellectual seduction, and she was far too young.

She answered by flinging her hands upward and opening the

fingers slowly, like lily petals unfolding. Struggling for the right words, she found none and let her hands fall as she lowered her blushing face.

"I understand," said Victor Lytle, while the younger children sat wide-eyed, feeling the charged atmosphere like a sudden heat on their skins and not knowing what caused it.

I tried to catch Peter's eye, but when I did, he raised one eyebrow in wonderment at why I should want to. As far as he was concerned, nothing had happened. How strange, when Laura was his darling. His greatest pleasure was hearing her play the bogus Stradivarius she had long outgrown.

In a few days, Edward Parmeter called to learn how his protégé was fitting into our family.

"He is a very pleasant, well-bred young man. Just how is he related to you?"

"He's what we southerners call a kissin' cousin," he said and laughed sardonically when I stiffened at the term. "Madame, don't you even let yourself think of such matters? I have enjoyed many dream kisses in my time, and I beg you not to deprive yourself of such pleasure!"

I turned away quickly, wondering where the children were. They always tumbled about my skirts when I had callers, the younger ones, at least, and while I didn't always appreciate this, I would have been glad for their presence now.

As if Edward had read my mind, he said, "Do you realize that this is the first time I have seen you minus your clutch of children? Without them, you seem like a girl."

"I am not a girl, and you must excuse me now. I must see to supper. Peter likes to sit down the minute the clock strikes six."

Edward bowed with that tight, crooked smile of his and pulled something from his pocket. "Speaking of Peter, he sent this from the store. A napkin ring for your guest."

As I took the silver band from its tissue paper, I saw the engraved name, "Victor Lytle," and shrank from its message of permanence. Victor was encroaching upon me and mine in some indefinable way, and I wanted it to stop. Suddenly I wanted him out of my house.

After showing Edward out, I went looking for the children. As I rounded the house, I could see them in the grape arbor, glimpse their sun-dappled faces through heavy bunches of ripe and near-ripe concords.

Stig sat on Victor's knee, Kamille was in the curve of his arm, Valborg sat at his feet, and Else had climbed up behind him to lace her arms loosely around his neck while she rested one cheek on the top of his head. Above the droning of bees feasting on bursted grapes, Victor's voice intoned the fable of the fox and the grapes. Though his eyes sought each small, rapt face in turn, he was performing for Laura, who sat opposite with her hands folded in the lap of the new gingham dress she should have changed when she came home from school.

As I looked at her, I knew that she was unaware of Victor as a man. Her dreamy gaze moved out along the row of carriage houses along the back of our block. Her wonder was inchoate, as mine had been before Jette's revelations crystallized it to a degree, and I knew the pain and pleasure of it. No parent could give this gauzy glory its form, but Peter and I must keep her dreaming in it until the time was right for someone else to do so. Not Victor!

Peter thought I exaggerated, and with his support, Victor stayed to teach Laura the Greek myths and fill her childish slate with the names of the Olympians. It was Danae's shower of gold, and I was not surprised when Peter came to our room with the slate in his trembling hand.

"Look at this!" His voice broke and he turned his face away as I read "I love you" written in Victor Lytle's beautiful Spencerian hand.

"What did you say to her?" I asked.

He groaned. "I—I said, 'Do you like this man?' and she said, 'Yes, Papa.' " He paused for a deep breath and continued with effort, "I asked, 'Do you love this man?' and she—she said, 'Yes, Papa.' Then I asked—'Do you love him more than you love your father?' She—said—" He covered his face with his hands.

"Oh Peter—" I touched his shoulder and kissed his temple, the only spot missed by the covering hands. "I will ask Victor to leave our house."

"I've done that. He's gone."

"And Laura?"

"She's here—somewhere."

I found her in the arbor holding a book that Victor had given her. It was Homer's *Odyssey* in Greek. Her face was as still and terrible as if she had seen the Gorgon's head, but when she saw me, she let out a wail and ran to my arms. Such agony for one so young, I thought, hating Victor.

"How *could* Papa?" she sobbed, "Victor wanted to marry me!"

Too stunned to respond to what she had said, I picked up the book that had fallen to the ground.

"Child, you can't read Greek; why did he give you this?"

"Because he loved it best—and he was going to teach me— he was going to teach me everything!"

During the severe October cold snap of that year Laura took a chill. For days she coughed desperately, and we were just congratulating ourselves on her recovery, when she was taken by new chills. Then there was fever, headache, and pains in the neck and back. For safety's sake, I sent the other children to Lily.

Doctor Gus, who made the dread diagnosis of spinal meningitis, was helpless in the face of it. He swore and prayed alternately at her bedside while he applied useless remedies through an agonizing week of pain and delirium.

"She won't fight!" he groaned.

When Laura called Victor's name, he said, "Who's Victor?"

I explained, and he yelled, "For God's sake, get him here! We've tried everything else!"

Coming back to our house was a hard thing for Victor, and the fact that he came softened my anger toward him. When he approached Laura's bed, she opened her eyes wide.

"Laura, don't leave me!" He knelt, twining a tangled lock of her hair around his finger.

Her limp hand found his sleeve and her eyes were hot with love and fever. The air around them seemed to burn. I couldn't bear it, and Doctor Gus led me out of the room.

"Peter had better let her have her way about this," he said.

"Come with me to tell him!" I said, radiant with the hope his words had given me.

In his fierce need to be occupied, Peter had gone to the stable to groom Holger. Seeing us, he threw down the curry comb and hurried forward. "Well? Well? How is she?"

"She'll live if she can love," Doctor Gus said simply. "I've seen it happen time and again."

"God damn him!" Peter shouted, "Our *blomster pige* is too good for him!"

"She doesn't want to live without him. Please, Peter—" I ran my hand down his arm and clasped his fingers, "Go in and tell her it's all right."

He stood for a moment like a stone, then strode into the house, into the sick room. How cold he was as he touched her hair and said, "Marry him if you must." He left the room without acknowledging Victor's presence.

Those grudging words were miraculous medicine. Laura recovered slowly but steadily, and Peter in his elation chose to forget what he had said on the crucial day. While Laura relied on her father's promise, she avoided unpleasantness by seeing Victor during the business day when Peter was occupied at the Beehive.

Theirs was a strange time of betrothal, but Laura and Victor were supremely happy. They wanted to set a wedding date immediately, but I begged for time to transform a convalescent school girl into a bride.

I also begged Victor to let Laura finish school before they were married, but he said, "I will teach her more than she'll ever learn here!"

Laura caught my hand, adding her own plea, "Oh yes, Mama, he makes even the dull things seem wonderful! Please?"

I remembered how poorly I had learned from Peter on our wedding journey and shook my head doubtfully.

My reaction brought tears to Laura's eyes, and she wilted as if the dread sickness were returning to pull her away. She was a fine little actress, I thought wryly, but her performance served to remind me that a promise must be kept.

"We can't be ready before late September—" I said.

They protested and argued for mid-summer, but I stood firm, bracing for the task of telling Peter.

Peter shouted, roared, and pounded the table. "I won't stand for it!"

"You promised her." I dropped the words like three cold stones.

He gave me a silent, terrible look. I was the enemy.

"Would you rather see her dead than married to Victor?" The harsh words hurt me, but they had to be said.

He turned his back on me, but I saw the unclenching of his hands.

Peter was absently polite throughout the preparations for the wedding. He was pleasant to Mrs. Oxler when she came to the house to fit Laura's gown, and he took the younger children to the store to give me a chance to make the house spotless and shining for the great occasion. All this he did, but he scarcely spoke to Laura.

The tiny slip of myrtle I had wrapped in damp moss to bring to America had flourished through the years, and as I was weaving a bridal crown from its glossy, green leaves, Laura came to me and said, "Do you think Papa ever will forgive me?"

"If you are happy with Victor, he'll have to."

"But we're going so far—all the way to Virginia. How will he ever know?"

With a pang at the thought of this parting, I said, "I will know, and I will tell him—again and again until he knows too."

I placed the crown on her hair, and she surrendered her sorrow as she advanced to meet her smiling mirror image. She was lovely.

Laura and Victor stood before the snowdrift of Brussels lace at the south parlor windows listening to the final instructions of the Christian Church pastor.

Mrs. Oxler had outdone herself, but I saw our *blomster pige* through a mist of tears that transformed her bridal gown of tucked lace into a simple frock she wore as a child in Ribe.

Too young! And yet as Victor bent to whisper to her, that radiant, up-turned face belonged to a woman.

I blinked away the tears and told Stig to stop fidgeting. It was time to begin.

"Dearly beloved, we are gathered..."

Then, "I, Laura Jorgen, take thee..." How clearly she spoke.

And as Victor promised "to love and to cherish..." I knew he would keep his vow. Until this moment, I had assented to the marriage as a matter of honor, but now I loved Victor because he loved Laura.

During the ceremony, Peter was coldly controlled, stiff as a palace guard, but when Laura put on her bonnet to run to the carriage with Victor, he stood in her way and seized her in a bone-crushing embrace. When they were gone, he returned to the guests with a brittle cordiality.

"It was so beautiful, Amalie!" Lily Hertert said.

"Yes," I said happily, "it was!"

My hostess duties kept me from Peter for some time, and when there was a lull, he was nowhere to be seen.

Much later I crept to the stable door to find him hanging on Holger's neck and groaning, "Oh God! Oh God!"

Fathers and daughters.

20

We took up our life again as if there had been a death in the family. Peter seemed inconsolable, and I couldn't help him, for he wouldn't come to me for comfort.

Else moved into Laura's tiny bedroom to remove the curse of its emptiness, but I would always forget and set Laura's place at the table.

Stig started wetting the bed again, a habit Peter had broken by dousing him with a pail of water every time he had an accident. Now Peter didn't notice or care.

We said little to each other in the constrained atmosphere of the house, and one day Valborg said, "Mama, is it always going to be like this?"

"Like what?" I asked dully.

"You and Papa just aren't here! Kamille thinks you went away with Laura..." Her eyes squeezed shut to stop the tears, which only forced the bright droplets out over her round cheeks.

"*Lille* Valborg..." I pulled her to me and pressed my face into hair that had gone unwashed for too long. There was a demarcation between the washed and unwashed portions of her neck and a rip in the shoulder of her dress.

I really looked at her and saw that I too had been paralyzed by Peter's suffering.

"I'm back," I whispered.

That night I told Peter what Valborg had said, and he set his jaw as he had done after the Ribe fire.

"Put on their coats, Amalie."

"But it's time for them to go to bed!"

"Never mind that." He strode to the parlor, calling to the children with such a good imitation of joviality that I was nearly taken in. "Valborg, Else, Kamille, Stig! We are going for a ride!"

"At night, Papa?" Else asked, round-eyed.

"Never put off until tomorrow what you can do today," he said, tousling heads as he rounded them up.

Bewildered, they advanced, one at a time, to take the coats I held out, and I could see their gladness igniting from the spark of this unusual privilege.

Peter quickly harnessed the horses, and soon we were rolling over the brick streets, passing through soft pools of gaslight at the corners.

"Where are we going?" I asked.

"To the Beehive. Everyone shall have a treat."

Those horehound drops, peppermint pillows, licorice whips, and chunks of rock candy scarcely paid for weeks of parental neglect, but children clasp joy without quibbling and take it as the promise of more.

With a single lamp lighted over the counter, the aisles were shadowy with specters. I could almost see Laura fingering the yard goods, dreaming of a new dress, until the other children broke the illusion with a noisy game of tag.

Then Edward Parmeter burst through the front door with the decrepit night watchman in tow.

"Peter! It's you! I thought we were being robbed!"

I had not seen Edward since Laura's wedding. In the flickering light of the lamp he looked jaded and tired. He had had his losses too, I thought with an unusual stirring of sympathy. Perhaps Edward really had loved Lily's niece, Elizabeth, or the girl who came after, another teacher named Mary Bartlet, but neither would stay in Harlan to be his wife. He must be very lonely. Impulsively I asked him to have supper with us the next night.

He glanced over at Peter, who was carefully locking the strongbox after putting in the money for the children's treats.

"You're very kind, ma'am, but I try not to tantalize myself with what I can't have."

"You mustn't say that! You'll have a family of your own someday."

"What a maddening woman you are!" he said in a low voice, then added a louder good-night to Peter and the children.

His words and the secret look that accompanied them filled me with a pleasurable confusion, for which I presently flayed myself. Would I never grow up? No matter how hard experience struck me, I never seemed to gain Mor's dignified serenity or Bedstemor Stine's wry good sense. I sat close to Peter and slid my arm through his as we drove home, wanting to be claimed and saved from something I wouldn't name.

The breath of the horses rose in clouds of steam, the weight of Stig's sleeping head pressed my thigh, and the girls chattered behind us in licorice- and peppermint-scented words.

"Look!" Kamille cried, "Feathers in the sky!"

"That's snow, silly!" Else said.

"Let her call it what she likes," said Valborg; "things don't look the same to everybody."

And what would I call the first snowfall? A blotter for the wearying estrangements of the last weeks; a mantle of assuaged pride settling on Peter's shoulders as he returned to us.

As the flakes fell cool on my face, I said, "Peter, I love you!"

"Of course you do," he said, and when the children were put to bed, we made love.

Through the years I had taken little note of the subtle changes in both of us since our wedding day, but that night I felt how deeply my fingers sank into Peter's back when I embraced him and grieved for the lost firmness of breasts that had nursed seven babies.

"Peter, are we getting old?"

"Only ripe and delicious like Graasten apples at picking time!"

How good it was to be wife first and mother after! I fell asleep pressed against Peter's back, unafraid of the time that measured itself by the beating of his heart beneath my hand.

On Thanksgiving Day we heard a late morning sermon on our manifold blessings, then drove to the community feast at the Harlan House. We considered this American holiday which had no exact counterpart in Denmark a most joyous occasion, though we did not join in all the festivities. When the dining hall was cleared for dancing, we turned our backs on the waltz, the schottische, and the polka, and went home to lift the burner lids from the kitchen stove for chestnut roasting.

Though Peter had been shocked at our church's prohibition of dancing, he abided by it, saying, "Since I did not think to ask about such matters before I was one of them, I cannot complain now. Dancing certainly would not harm us, but we must not be a scandal to the brethren."

Stage plays were another matter, and Peter saw no inconsistency in scandalizing the brethren by attending an amateur performance of *The Merchant of Venice*. I did not call it to his attention, for Lily Hertert had been cast in the role of Portia, and I meant to see her play it no matter whom we offended. I planned to take Valborg and Else to the performance, for they worshipped Lily. She always spoke to them as if they shared her broad knowledge, which sent them flying to learn what she thought they knew already.

Peter engaged four of the best seats in the Opera House, and Mrs. Oxler made new dresses for me and the older girls. Mine was deep blue taffeta with white ruching at the throat, Valborg's was garnet silk with jet beads that I considered too old for her, and Else's was cream with a pale blue sash. The gaslights flickered on similar finery all over the packed house, and the girls, who never had seen such massed elegance, were speechless with admiration and proud to be a part of it all.

The maroon velvet curtains opened on a crudely painted Venetian street, and we sat impatiently through the faltering first scene, waiting for Lily.

She was worth waiting for. The years had brought a cooler glint to her pale hair, subtly silvering a strand here and there, and there was a slight thickening beneath her chin, but as she entered and said, "By my troth, Nerissa, my little body is aweary of this great world," she was so much the Venetian maiden that I forgot I was watching a friend whose plum-colored robe was her library curtain, replaced two years before and packed away in camphor balls.

"Oooh!" Else breathed, pushing up in her seat to see over the high-puffed hair of Mrs. Nicolai, the wife of the livery stable owner.

Lily's performance seemed as good as many I had seen in Copenhagen, possibly because she was so much better than the other players.

Belle McGuire, the wife of the Harlan House proprietor, played Nerissa. When she entered in male garb, she was not recognized by the audience, but when Lily strode on in the guise of the young doctor from Rome, her identity was unmistakable. People around us gasped at the display of her full, well-formed legs in tights and scarcely recovered in time for her "quality of mercy" speech.

"Isn't she fine?" Peter whispered over the heads of the girls, and I came very close to defining the jealousy that tinged my love for Lily. The footlights glowed on a woman who had climbed to the rooftops and stayed there, while I had scuttled down.

After the play we joined the long line waiting outside Lily's dressing room to congratulate her. John Hertert came out to announce that she would be dressed in a few minutes.

"Lily was wonderful!" Peter told him.

"I wish she'd stop making a fool of herself," John growled, "I'm going out back to smoke a cigar until this nonsense is over!"

"How nasty of him!" I whispered to Peter.

"He doesn't mean it, he just wants her all to himself. But he doesn't know how to handle her."

"Would any man?"

He gave me a startled look. "Of course! You're just like her in many ways, but *you* stay where you belong."

My angry retort was lost in the excitement of Lily's reappearance. Still smelling strongly of greasepaint, she put her arms around me and whispered, "How wonderful that you could come! How did you ever arrange it with the Puritans?" Then she was pulling roses from the bouquet John had sent to give to the girls, and we were pushed along by the others who wanted a word with her.

The next day two ladies from the church called to remonstrate with me for "encouraging the Devil's pastime." When I explained that seeing the play was a debt of friendship, they were slightly mollified and agreed to take a cup of elderberry tea in the parlor.

"They say she showed her legs!" Mrs. Lehigh murmured darkly.

"God made them," I said.

"But not for that!"

"Do have another almond cookie," I said. "I baked them this morning."

"The Bible says it's wrong for a woman to get herself up like a man," said Mrs. Carmichael.

"Lily was only play-acting," I said, which turned the conversation back to the Devil's pastime. I listened meekly, and when those good women departed, they were sure they had snatched a brand from the burning.

Not long afterward, a greater scandal put Lily's brief thespian career in the shade. H. Bates, the owner of a rival general store, fell sick and was discovered to be a woman.

It was January, and the heavy snow had drifted and packed so hard that horse-drawn cutters replaced carriages, even in town. We had a new one, and I had it out for the first time when I saw Doctor Gus approaching from the opposite direction and hailed him, eager as a child wanting to show off a new toy. He did not acknowledge my greeting but stared straight ahead, the reins slack in his hands. He had just learned what the rest of us were to know later, though, of course, the story did not come from him.

Ada Christophersen told it around. She was H. Bate's long-spurned neighbor, and as soon as she recognized Doctor Gus's cutter next door, she hurried over with a bowl of hot soup. She arrived in time to hear the doctor explode, "My God! You're a woman!"

"Keep it to yourself or I'll cut your tongue out!" H. Bates

spoke with a mighty, wheezing effort, for her lungs were filling fast. "Who the hell asked you to come here?"

"Your clerks at the store said you were home sick, and there hasn't been a wisp of smoke from your chimney for two days. Are you trying to kill yourself?"

"Get out!" cried H. Bates.

"My oath won't let me," Doctor Gus said, stamping toward the kitchen to start a fire in the stove.

Ada Christophersen was out the back door before her presence was discovered, and when she saw that she still had the soup bowl in her hands, she turned right around and knocked as if she were just arriving.

"Doctor Gus didn't let on that the whole business was anything out of the ordinary, " she reported, "and you could see his breath right in that room! That was the first time I ever set foot in the Bates house, and it sure doesn't look like any woman lived there! No curtains and not one pretty thing! I asked Doctor Gus if I could help any way, and he said he'd let me know and shut the door in my face. Doesn't that beat all?"

It did indeed. Peter and Edward had made many buying trips with H. Bates, sharing the same hotel room, and when I asked Peter how such a secret could be kept, he said, "He—I mean she—always slept in long underwear and never shared a bed, but otherwise, there wasn't a clue. She drank, swore, smoked cigars and played cards like a man, and no man in town is shrewder in business!"

As for her name, the townspeople had amused themselves for years by guessing what the initial *H* stood for: Horace, Henry, Harold, Hermes? The guessing game now took on new fascination with Hortense, Henrietta, Hattie, and Hepzibah as possibilities.

No factual information about H. Bates existed, for she had no confidants and never spoke of her past. In Harlan, as in the other settlements of this young country, personal questions were avoided out of a reluctance to stand in the way of a fresh start for anyone fleeing a disgraceful or hopeless past.

The station master remembered that H. Bates had come in on the train ten years earlier, someone else reported that she paid spot cash for the store and her house, and a barber recalled that she always refused a shave, but no one could say, "I always knew it!" H. Bates was tall with a deep voice and a flat chest, and her habits were as masculine as those of any man in town, with the exception of a total lack of interest in women.

I was as curious as anyone, but when I drove to the small house on Farnam street with a covered dish of dumplings, I took one look at the line of food-bearing women and went away shamed. Whatever torment had driven her to live as a man was her secret. Let others pry it from her if they must, but I would not.

No one ever did, for pneumonia took the life of H. Bates before a single caller could be admitted to her house. When the ground thawed enough to yield to a spade, she lay in the Harlan cemetery with the mysterious *H* chiseled in her headstone, a riddle for all time.

21

That summer we moved back to the farm and Peter took his first real vacation from the store to supervise the digging of a new well and to teach Stig to sit a horse properly.

We were unused to spending an entire day together, except for Sundays, which were laden with unnatural prohibitions. Children were kept in their Sunday clothes until bedtime. Running, shouting, and reading anything other than the Holy Bible was forbidden, and the long hours were filled with antiphonal yawns. Americans had it backwards, I thought, behaving as if man were made for the Sabbath.

Spring had lingered that year, and we began the cool days of June with leisurely breakfast in a bower of prairie flowers picked by the children.

"Are you happy, Amalie?" Peter asked.

I considered, taking inventory of a handsome, provident husband; healthy surviving children; a house as fine as most in Harlan; a country place; and enough friends to allow me to shape my life in its telling.

"I think so, though it tempts fate to say it. Why do you ask?"

"Because I feel so happy today! If I step out, I may find one foot in Audubon County! Everything is growing—the children, the corn, the profits from the store—"

"And from the grain elevator, " I added, recalling the incident that had given Peter the reputation of Solomon a few weeks before.

Peter had taken over the management of the elevator during the winter, and by April, oats were disappearing in a quantity that no horde of rats could devour. Peter stayed at the elevator all night to solve the mystery, but the thief seemed to know that he was there and did not appear. Finally Peter set a beaver trap and covered it with oats. The next day, he stopped a worker who limped as he never had done before. The steel teeth of the trap matched the wounds on the man's leg. As soon as the confession was out, Peter drove the thief to Doctor Gus's office for treatment.

When he came home, he said, "I should have taken the loss. That was too cruel! I am ashamed!"

"It was not the money, Peter, but your pride. You know you can't bear to let anyone get the best of you!"

"It will be a cold day in July before anyone tries again!"

Now Peter rose from the table and went to the door. "Here comes your new well!"

The Yankee well-digger was driving his rig into the farmyard. He was to sink a new well conveniently close to my kitchen, and even if the water ran deep as the center of the earth, Peter meant to bring it up.

The well-digger had stubby legs overbalanced by a powerful torso, and he had to tilt his head to look into Peter's face. A red handkerchief tied around his head Apache style kept the sweat from his eyes, and his clothes were stained by the labor of many days. Dirty and ugly as he was, I took pleasure in the sight of him, for he was bringing release from the long walk to the well beyond the upper barns.

As I watched through the window, he started to argue with Peter. He flung his arm toward the barns, pointed to the spot where we wanted him to dig, and shook his head.

"I don't care what you say," Peter shouted, "that well is to be sunk right here!"

"You're a fool if you do it!"

"That's not for you to judge!" Peter roared. "If you won't do it, I'll hire someone else!"

"A fool's money is as good as any other man's," the well-digger said. He clucked to his horse and the half-blind old creature brought up his rig. The well-digger spat on the ground and went to work.

Lily Hertert came to call a few afternoons later, stepping daintily around the mound of excavated earth near the kitchen door.

"I have the most marvelous idea, Amalie," she said. "Let me take the children back to town and pretend they're mine while you have Peter with you. It's time you two were re-acquainted, don't you think?"

"Peter and I have no need for the children's absence," I said, "Danish fathers do not permit children to interfere with their lives."

Lily sighed and fanned herself. "You're making this very hard for me. Must I come right out and confess that it was a selfish suggestion? I *want* them! Having none of my own has been the hardest condition of my life!"

Though I had gathered as much, Lily never had put her yearning into words, and I could think of no reason to refuse her. Else had overheard, and her big, expressive eyes were begging silently behind Lily's back.

When Peter came in for his afternoon coffee, I explained the matter to him, and he was agreeable, so off the children went to a promised supper at the Harlan House. Lily's face glowed beneath her wide-brimmed hat as she drove away with all four of them leaning on her and mussing her white dimity dress.

Peter and I were ill-at-ease in the strangely silent house, and I pondered Lily's words about getting re-acquainted. I no longer remembered how to cook for two, and I set six places at the table before I realized there was no need.

At sundown, the well-digger knocked on the door to inform us that he had finished. "It's Chinese water you'll be gettin', but it's there," he said, spitting on the ground and wiping his mouth with his forearm.

The new rope unreeled interminably before the wooden bucket struck water with a muffled splash. Peter turned the crank until his forehead beaded with sweat to bring it to the surface. He offered me the first drink from the blue enamel dipper. It was cold and good, with a faint taste of iron.

"Chinese water!" I said with a laugh, "Wonderful!"

Both of us drank quantities of it in the days that followed, for we had only to step outside to raise a pailful. The novelty of it fascinated us, and we particularly appreciated the convenience during several days of heavy June rains when the long trip to the upper well would have been difficult.

I knew that Peter had a fever before he did. I sponged him with cool vinegar water and made him lie still. His skin was hot as a stovepipe in winter, but I expected it to cool as evening came on.

He was a poor patient, loudly insisting that nothing was wrong with him and pushing my vinegar cloths away. I had done my share of nursing the sick, and I never had dealt with anyone so cross and cantankerous. I told him so.

"It is an insult to be sick!" he raged, "I won't have it!"

"Well, you do have it, so lie back and be still!" As I pushed him against the pillows, the opening of his nightshirt gapped, and I pulled in my breath at the sight of rose-colored spots on his chest.

"Give me the chamber pot and go away!" he groaned.

I did as he asked, worrying over the glimpse I had of him clutching his stomach with no thought for his usual modest tenting of the necessary object with his nightshirt.

"I'm going for Doctor Gus," I called through the door, and when he didn't protest, I was more frightened than ever. He thought doctors were for women and children, only to be resorted to by men in the most extreme circumstances.

Not wanting to take the time to harness Holger, Peter's bay, I mounted Ophelia, the old drayhorse Berg had left tied to the fence. Her splayfooted gait had all the speed of a glacier. I had saved a few minutes and lost half an hour by my choice, I thought disgustedly, kicking her fat sides as I wiped my hot face with the tail of my shirt.

Riding Ophelia bareback was like straddling a hot stove. The miles seemed endless, and the sun was nearly down when I reached the outskirts of Harlan.

Doctor Gus would not be in his office at this hour, I reasoned, so I rode straight to his house on Seventh street. His horse was eating from a nosebag, still harnessed to the rig, which meant the doctor had evening calls to make.

Painfully conscious of the thick dust on my skin, clothes, and hair, I hoped the neighbors were not looking out their windows as I slid from Ophelia's back and fumbled with the gate latch. It seemed to blur and move when I reached for it. A lace curtain swayed at the front window, and the doctor's wife, Minna, hurried down the walk to help me in.

Doctor Gus came into the hall chewing, followed by his young son.

"It's Peter—" A great roaring in my ears mingled with a sense of falling.

When Doctor Gus's features re-formed before my eyes, I supposed I was still in his house, irrelevantly noticing that Minna had chosen the same wallpaper that I had put in the farmhouse bedroom.

"You must go to Peter—"

"He's in the next room. Better off than you are," Doctor Gus told me, and I saw that I was in Laura's bed.

"What—" a terrible stomach pain stopped my question, but I did not have to repeat it.

"Typhoid," said Doctor Gus. "You couldn't have found a worse place to put a well, and I can't understand how you found anyone dumb enough to dig it for you! For that matter, *you* should have known that you can't let all that barnyard pollution run down into your water supply!"

"Peter knows nothing of farms, and Far's buildings in the Old Country were on the flat," I said miserably, remembering Peter's argument with the Yankee well-digger and my delight in his triumph.

"Our main problem now is finding somebody to take care of you. People are scared of typhoid, and I couldn't hire you a nurse for a hundred dollars a day, but you've got to have one! *I* have a few other things to do."

"How—how long have you been here?"

"Two days now. I left once to deliver a baby. It was Mrs. Dinesen, and thank God they come fast for her!"

"I can get up and take care of things," I said, but when I tried to swing my legs from the bed, I knew it was an idle boast. I fell back and cried in my weakness.

"Come on, you're no weeper!" Doctor Gus said. "Now you just stay put and I'll find somebody to ease you through this."

"But—but you said you couldn't—not for a hundred dollars a day."

"There's a woman who might do it. She lives all alone down by the tracks and most folks are scared of her. They call her a witch, but that's nonsense! She lost all her babies with diphtheria one winter a long time ago and her husband ran off, and if that isn't enough to make a person peculiar, I'd like to know what is! Want me to ask her?"

"Oh yes— please—"

"And have your man board up that well! It's only by the grace of God that your children didn't drink from it!"

"Does Lily know what—what we have?"

He nodded. "She'll keep your brood until you can take them back. It's a funny thing—even an woman as intelligent as Lily is terrified of typhoid, but I guess I can't say much. My own wife gets a funny look in her eye when you mention it, and she burned the rug you fell on in the hall the other night."

"I feel like a leper!"

"Well, don't. Just concentrate on getting well. You'll have to watch what you eat for a long time, and I'll tell Clarine what you can have."

After the doctor left, I called out to Peter, reverting to Danish in my distress, "This is like the plague of the Middle Ages! What will become of us?"

He answered in English. We'll come through! I refuse to give myself to such a mean death!"

"At least the children are safe," I sighed, writhing in the same misery that Peter was experiencing on the other side of the wall. Holding his hand would have helped, but I would give up that comfort rather than have Peter see me in the throes of this ugly illness. I knew he would not want me to see him so. He was a proud man.

When Clarine Reed came to us, I could see why the people in

town called her a witch. She was old and stooped with a squint that must appear sinister to those who had no way of knowing her essential kindness.

She seldom spoke, and when she did, her voice was rough and grating, as if her vocal cords had rusted from long disuse, but her bony hands were gentle when they lifted my head to freshen the pillows, and she was a good, plain cook.

Clarine disposed of the bloody contents of the chamber pots with no show of repugnance and obligingly delivered the notes Peter and I wrote to each other to pass the time.

"You may read them if you wish, Clarine," I told her on the day when I belatedly realized she might think we were using this means to talk about her behind her back.

"That's kindly taken, Mrs. Jorgen, but it wouldn't do me no good. I can't read. For a long time, that was a sorrow to me, but I've finally lived long enough to take what comes without frettin'."

"I'll *never* live that long!" I cried, fretting that very moment over the long, slow convalescence. I yearned to see the children. The letters they wrote under Lily's guidance were precious but insufficient. Doctor Gus reported that Lily held the pages we wrote to them with an old sugar tongs to avoid infection.

Clarine was off to the upper well, two pails swinging from the yoke across her shoulders. Watching her through the window, I wondered how we could ever repay her for the risk she had discounted. Doctor Gus said there was no danger, but no one believed him, least of all Clarine, who had no use for learning.

Then I started a new note to Peter, all rambling nonsense about the old days. Beginning in curly, Danish script, I soon switched to English, for most of my thoughts were in the new language now. I had learned it with great difficulty, and as my mastery grew, I thought of ways to teach it to someone else, devising what I thought were simplifications to help a struggling novice. Why couldn't I teach Clarine to read? If I could offer her that magnificent gift, our account would be squared!

Crumpling Peter's note, I made the letters of the English alphabet in a column along the left margin of a fresh page. Then I began to draw pictures beside each letter: an apple for *A,* a striped bumblebee for *B,* an ocean wave for *C,* and then the system broke down. I could think of no picture for *D* nor for any of the letters that followed until I reached *I.* I started again, trying to illustrate the various sounds of the letters, but my ideas outran my artistry, and I wished for Valborg.

Well, no matter. There must be some way to teach Clarine to read—if she wanted it as much as I believed she must. As soon as she returned from the well, I broached the subject.

She threw up both hands. "Oh no, Mrs. Jorgen, I couldn't! I'm too old, and it doesn't matter. I've learned to do without."

"But wouldn't you like to read your own letters? And the newspaper? What about your Bible?"

"Nobody in this world ever writes to me, and I've stopped caring what other people do—except you and the Mister, that is. As far as the Bible goes, I went to church a good many years, and I learned the best parts by heart—like 'For God so loved the world that he gave his only begotten Son—' I ain't got the head for reading."

In my eagerness to convince her that reading wasn't all that difficult, I tried to get out of bed to look for the children's primers, but I didn't have the strength to get past the bedroom door.

Clarine humored me by finding the books and sitting beside my bed with a glazed and respectful look while I tried to teach her a few simple words by rote. This went on for days, and though I worked with her until the two of us were exhausted, she couldn't tell *cat* from *boy.*

"I just ain't got the head for it," she apologized, and Peter, on his feet for the first time with the aid of a cane, looked in on us with amusement.

"Don't be so proud, Amalie," he said. "Give up. Clarine knows her limitations better than you do."

Clarine's grateful eyes thanked him as she escaped with the offer to bring us custard.

"If she would only believe that she could do it!" I exploded.

"Exactly, but she doesn't, and she never will. You're only making her unhappy with all this tutoring. Will you never learn to accept people as they are?"

"Have *you?*" I challenged.

"Yes, I accept them as they are when I know they can do no more."

"Only God knows when that is!" I said, but I put the primers away, and Clarine's relief was visible.

We cannot always choose the coin with which we pay our debts.

22

The weakening effects of typhoid depressed Peter, but he bore them with grace and even a certain dash. Dependent on a cane, he ordered one of carved teak with an ornate, brass head, and soon young dandies with no disability were imitating him.

Every day at noon I would send one of the children to the Beehive with a bland, dull lunch I had packed for him, and he would take it from their hands as if they had brought him a feast.

I was tired all the time, and while I did not walk with a cane, I held to the furniture as I moved about the house. I had asked Clarine to come and live with us when we returned to town, but she would not leave her shack near the depot, and the responsibility for running the house was on Valborg's shoulders. The stamp of her personal disorder was everywhere: crooked rugs, baskets of unironed laundry, and scattered books and papers.

"This can't go on!" Peter fumed, "I will find you someone."

That someone was Dorrit Ancher, a girl from North Jutland who brought me the accents of home and a hard-working thrift to gladden the heart.

The house on Willow street sparkled beneath her hand, and Peter and I were encouraged to begin a round of long-neglected entertaining. Though Dorrit's spicy Danish cooking was forbidden to us, we enjoyed offering it to our friends. On one of our evenings we would seat twenty-four at table, where some of the guests would remain after the meal because the parlor would not hold them all.

Noting that our invitations went to Peter's lodge brothers and business acquaintances and their wives, most of them Yankees, Dorrit bluntly asked my why we saw so little of our own people. She herself had made rapid friendships in the Danish community.

"Peter never puts his feet in two boats," I told her; "he is an American now."

Kamille burst into the kitchen and interrupted us as no well-behaved Danish child would. "Mama, will you listen to my poem? If I have to say it for the company, I have to get it right."

"Go ahead, Kamille," I said, smiling at the way she planted her high-buttoned shoes wide apart with the toes turned inward.

Pulling in a huge breath, she gravely announced, " 'Over The Hill to The Poor-House' by Will M. Carleton. 'Over the hill to the poor-house I'm trudgin' my weary way—I, a woman of seventy, and only a trifle gray . . . . ' "

Dorrit listened soberly to the self-pitying account of a woman rejected by all her ungrateful children, understanding little of Kamille's breathless recital, but catching its doleful tone. When it was finished, she asked, "Is that how it is in America?"

"It's just a poem, Dorrit," I laughed, but I did wish Kamille had chosen something else to recite. I was not partial to Will M. Carleton's maudlin pathos, though it enjoyed great popularity among our acquaintances.

That night when Kamille gave her real performance, Mrs. Nicolai wept openly and several of the ladies dabbed at their eyes surreptitiously while the men listened with feigned interest, eager to get on with their discussion of politics and lodge affairs.

Grover Cleveland was sure to make his second bid for the presidency, and Peter favored him, but most of our guests were Republican, which would force him, as a good host, to suppress his views.

Soon the gathering separated by gender, and the rooms resounded with interwoven conversations. The older men refought the battle of Pittsburgh Landing, the lodge brothers discussed the handsome emblematic carpet they had just bought, and Roger Lucas defended high tariffs in ringing tones while Peter bit his lips to hold back refutation.

The women talked about recipes for glycerine and rose water lotion and a new washing machine that would keep their hands out of hot wash water altogether, if they could trust it to do the job, which they would not.

I saw a flash of garnet silk at the door to the kitchen. What was Mrs. Nicolai doing out there? I waited until she was back in the parlor, then went to speak to Dorrit about the late evening refreshments we always offered our guests in addition to dinner.

Slicing a rolled loaf of spiced meat with deadly efficiency, Dorrit said, "She asked me to come to her. She said she would pay me more."

"What did you tell her?"

"That I would stay with my own kind—even if you *are* more Yankee than Dane!"

"Oh Dorrit, I am no longer one thing nor the other! I think I will always be divided in my heart. Do you understand?"

She considered and finally nodded slowly, "Someday I may look around me and say to this country, 'I wish you were my native land, for then my heart could be quiet'—someday I may do that."

We clasped hands, and our fingers slipped in the fat from the meat, making us laugh. When I returned to the parlor, Mrs. Nicolai avoided my eyes.

Through Dorrit I heard all the news of the Danish community, and one of the most interesting bits was the adoption of a five-year-old Chinese orphan by Steffen Secher and his wife Marthe.

The boy's parents had sickened and died near Cuppy's Grove without communicating where they had come from or where they were going. The meager possessions the couple had strapped to their backs held no information about them, and the little boy could not or would not speak.

The Sechers were in their 40's and childless. They took the boy and named him Ansgar for the saint who brought Christianity to the Danes. They were teaching him both Danish and English.

Ansgar Secher, with eyes like polished black stones and skin the color of a ripening peach, was the wonder of the countryside. I saw him once, waiting in the supply wagon outside the Beehive, and when I smiled at him, he said, *"God dag, gamle fru!"*

Old? I was startled by his use of the term, but to him I must have seemed old. I was thirty-three, old enough to have children as accomplished as Else, who shone at the spelling schools so popular that season.

The avid following of the spelling schools would brave the worst snowstorm to watch a champion spell down a field of contenders at the Opera House. Orchestra music, prizes, and applause added to the excitement of the competition.

The spellers sat in rows of chairs facing each other, the ladies on one side and the gentlemen on the other, and words were given to them alternately.

When Else rose to take her turn, the whole Jorgen family took one deep breath. She looked poised and confident in her ashes-of-roses best dress, excluding herself from our fear of the word that would come from the precise lips of the pronouncer.

"Lepidopterology," he said crisply, "a branch of entomology dealing with butterflies and moths."

I gasped, thinking Else couldn't possibly know how to spell it, but she calmly repeated the word and rattled out the letters in perfect order, smiling as she took her seat.

The next speller was Doctor Gus's son, Conrad. He seemed rattled. Stuttering "numismatist" after the pronouncer, he put an extra *i* in the word and retired to the audience.

Else spelled down fifteen contestants that night to win the grand prize, a Webster's unabridged dictionary, and we were too proud of her ourselves to begrudge her swelling self-importance. I could spell well enough in Danish, but English spelling still baffled me, and I was thrilled to have a child who could master it. Else's accomplishment led me on to rosy dreams of Kamille's recitations, Valborg's art, and Stig's great charm, as yet unchanneled. The Jorgens would contribute much to this country!

From the moment Peter heard about the Columbian Exposition in Chicago, he was wildly excited about going.

Seeing the "White City" built on the swampland of the South Side tempted me, but we still had to be careful about what we ate, and I wondered whether we could manage on restaurant food for as long as the journey would take. When I voiced my doubts, Peter scoffed at them.

"If need be, we'll buy a huge bunch of bananas and eat our way through the ideal city like a pair of monkeys!"

I could think of no other objections but the one I refused to mention. I had just been through a veiled explanation of female functions with Valborg, and this made me aware of recent differences in my own pattern. Had the typhoid brought on a premature change of life? I was embarrassed to ask Doctor Gus.

Mrs. Oxler had died just before Christmas, so I went to Clara Paup to be fitted for some dresses for the Exposition. When she read off my waist measurement, I told her that she must be mistaken. She measured again, and when she made me look for myself, I knew the cause of those extra inches. Change of life indeed!

Doctor Gus confirmed my pregnancy, and Peter was delighted.

"Anyone well enough to beget is well enough! Christian IV, we're catching up with you!"

I sighed. "Now I can't go to Chicago."

"I'll bring the Exposition back to you. I will notice all the little things that women like to know about and stagger home under the weight of souvenirs!"

A great deal happened in the three weeks he was gone. Peter and I never had gone back to the farm after our long, dreary illness there, and Berg Landsman came to town once in a great while to report on the condition of the land and buildings. The first time he saw Dorrit, he was attracted to her and she to him. They announced their intention to marry two days after Peter left, and I was desolate at the prospect of being without the girl. I was trying to rock away my agitation in the platform chair in our bedroom when she tapped lightly on the doorframe.

"Come in, Dorrit."

She hung back, twisting her hands in her apron until I repeated the invitation, then came to stand before me without raising her eyes.

"You look unhappy, Dorrit; that is no mood for a bride!"

"Pastor Sorensen will not marry us in the church."

Looking at Dorrit's rosy amplitude, I remembered the fierce intensity of Berg's longing beside the root cellar on a hot, sultry night a long time ago.

"I am so ashamed, Fru Jorgen! What shall I do?"

I caught my lower lip in my teeth, trying to think. The minister of the Christian Church was at least as harsh as Pastor Sorensen about such matters, and the Baptist minister was out of the question. Who then?

"Let me think, Dorrit. We'll work something out."

She went back to the kitchen to cut up noodles and I ground the crank on the new telephone Peter had had put in before he went away. After a long interval of popping and crackling on the line, Central answered, and I asked for Lily Hertert. We never bothered with numbers, just names. As I waited for Lily to answer her ring of one long and two shorts, I could hear receivers coming off the hook all along the line.

"Hertert's residence," Lily said dulcetly.

"Lily, this is Amalie. Can you come over? I need some advice."

"I suppose I'be better come to you—if I don't want to give it to the whole town!" She laughed, and several angry clicks were heard as the more sensitive eavesdroppers fell away.

When she arrived, I sent the children outside to play, and we solved Dorrit's problem in short order. Thomas Walker, the Justice of the Peace, would perform a brief ceremony in Lily's parlor with Lily and myself as witnesses, and a convenient vagueness about the whole affair would ensue. Even John and

Peter were not to know.

We chose Thursday, Dorrit's night out, when she could dress up and leave the house legitimately. As an explanation for my own departure in my best dress, I told Valborg that I was making a call of compassion and left her in charge of the younger children.

Lily's parlor was a bower of lilacs and tulips, which she had picked in frantic haste as soon as John's carriage rolled out of sight. White tapers glowed on the mantel, and Thomas Walker stood between them pulling at his collar. The clock struck nine, the appointed hour, but Berg and Dorrit were not forthcoming.

Lily frowned. "Do you suppose they changed their minds?"

I pulled the closed draperies aside and recognized the pale, awkward bulk of Ophelia near the hitching post.

"Berg is here, at least. Let me see what is happening."

I opened the front door narrowly to avoid presenting a recognizable silhouette to the neighbors and hurried to the lumber wagon.

"Berg," I whispered, "It's Amalie Jorgen. What's keeping you?"

Dorrit's moist whisper answered, "It's me, Fru Jorgen, I can't stop crying."

I pulled a handkerchief from my waistband and thrust it upward. "Come, we must be quick!"

They scrambled down and followed me, and as we all blinked in the sudden light of the foyer, I saw them rise within themselves to meet the elegance of Lily's house. Their love burned away all shame as they advanced to the mantel where Thomas Walker awaited them.

The utilitarian words of the civil ceremony were softened by the rosy globes of the lamps and the perfume of the lilacs, and I said a silent prayer for their happiness.

Dorrit blushed and trembled in her ecru and white striped dress, but Berg stood strong and solid as the great runic stone at Jelling. Both were beautiful in their seriousness, and as I looked at these two fine Danes through a film of tears, I saw Eden around them—...*male and female created he them*...

The candles on the mantel burned with a steady, upward flame, and as I kissed Dorrit's damp cheek, I called this to her attention as a good omen.

Berg shook my hand and looked long into my eyes, saying simply, "*Tak!*" Then they were gone.

In the morning, Dorrit was back in my kitchen, as we agreed she must be for a few days to cloud the circumstances. I didn't have to ask her how she was, for she was singing lustily as she pounded the beefsteak, "*Sim sala, dim sala*..." Even the children noticed and enjoyed her exceptionally high spirits.

Dorrit left at the end of the week to keep the farmhouse that had sheltered my joy and sorrow, and the Jorgens reverted to the haphazard way of life that Peter deplored. I could not believe that Dorrit's rigorously imposed order could vanish so quickly, and I threw myself into a frenzy of heavy cleaning.

Just then, a black-edged letter came from Ausig. Mor was dead.

With Peter gone, Lily was the logical source of comfort, and I went to her, but I came away unsatisfied. For Lily, immortality resided in the memories of other humans and in lasting deeds. For me, this was not enough.

I harnessed Holger to the small carriage and drove to the tiny, neat house that was Dagmar Jensen's Danish microcosm. I needed to be among my own people at this time, and Valborg's godmother would not turn me away.

She opened the door to me with a challenging look and called over her shoulder to the children, "Outside with you! A fine lady has come to call!"

Too distressed to be angry, I put out my hands. "Oh Dagmar, Mor is gone!"

Dagmar was a head shorter than I, but her arms managed to fold me in like a child. Through a long afternoon we talked in Danish over countless cups of coffee. I reviewed my life with Mor, probed the ways I had failed her, and spoke of her virtues in the language that was needed for this expression. I learned that I had not re-made my soul in its deepest reaches—that part of me would be Danish forever.

As we parted, Dagmar asked a searching question that whipped my pride to a negation of the comfort I had received.

"How is it that you come to us only in trouble?"

With such hard and stubborn countrymen, I had rather be a Yankee!"

23

Peter brought us the promised souvenirs from the Columbian Exposition: carved ivory elephants, folding fans, commemorative medals, and scale models of ornate buildings in the "White City."

"The spirit of regeneration is in Chicago!" he exulted, "When it spreads, this will be a beautiful land!"

Convinced that he no longer needed his cane, he had given it to a street beggar in Chicago, and he did walk with a quicker step now, but he was thin, and his eyes were unnaturally bright. He seemed to burn with a will to be healthy that had no basis in fact.

Edward Parmeter told me about the short, furtive naps Peter took in the back room of the store during the heat of the summer.

"Has Peter seen the doctor since he came back from Chicago?" he asked.

"No, but I'll suggest it," I said, wondering whether Edward's concern sprang from friendship or from pique at Peter's inability to shoulder his full share of the partnership responsibilities.

I telephoned Doctor Gus, asking him to come to the house that evening, and when he arrived with a blunt question, "Well, Peter, what's the complaint?" I wanted to run for cover.

"I didn't send for you!" Peter shouted, "I have no complaint!"

"Don't be a stubborn Dane!"

"I'm all right, I tell you! Now, either sit down and have a cup of coffee like a friend or get out of here!"

Doctor Gus looked at me and shrugged. "Cream and sugar, Amalie. By the way, how are *you* feeling?"

"Better than Peter!" I snapped, angry with him for refusing medical attention, but I brought the coffee and we spoke of other things. There had been talk of Peter running for the office of mayor. At first he had looked upon the suggestion as a joke, but he was considering it with increasing seriousness.

"Why don't you wait until you build yourself up a little?" Doctor Gus said, "There's plenty of time."

"Are you back to that again?" Peter flared, "Anything worth doing is worth doing immediately, and I tell you, I'm not sick!"

"Twenty years of medical practice tells me otherwise, but I suppose I'd have to knock you unconscious to treat you, and that involves some questionable medical ethics. Damn it, I wish we weren't friends! Excuse me, Amalie—" he bowed to me elaborately, spilling his untidy curls over his forehead.

"Excuse *me*, I have a lodge meeting," Peter said, making a stiff-backed exit.

"Don't let him run for that office," Doctor Gus told me.

"I can't stop him."

"Damn it!" he said without apology, rattling his cup down in its saucer.

When Peter came home much later, he announced, "I have

decided to offer myself to the voters."

I cried.

"Stop that!" he roared, "If this is the kind of support I have in my own household, what can I expect from others? Don't you think I can do the job?"

"Yes, but—"

"Put a period after the 'yes'!" he said sternly. Then he softened and raised my chin with his forefinger. "Amalie? Wouldn't you like to be Fru Mayor Jorgen?"

"I don't care," I said tearfully, "but I will stay on the rooftop with you."

"Rooftop? What are you saying?"

"Nothing. I was just thinking of an old tale."

"We'll write a new tale, one to make our children proud!"

The part that wives were to play in future campaigns had no place in the rigourous wooing of the male electorate in 1893, and I stayed at home, not knowing how Peter did in his political encounters, but certain that he would bring the charm of a Funen innkeeper to bear on the situation. Lily Hertert brought me John's report of a saloon rally, assuring me that Peter was running strong.

Strong until he stumbled through our door late at night and called for coffee. He would fall into an exhausted, twitching sleep before his cup was half empty.

"I can't bring the Danes to my side, Amalie," he said, "a Dane never likes to see one of his own surpass him."

"But our people don't want political office. They want somebody else to give them good government, and they'll work for whoever can do that."

"They call me a Yankee, then won't vote for me because I'm a Dane!" he said bitterly.

"Then you'll win on the Yankee votes!"

"We'll see. Thomas Walker is one of their own."

I visualized the dapper, little Justice of the Peace in the mayor's chair and decided that Peter would be much more imposing, even in his present debilitation.

This was the first time Peter had expressed a sense of separation from the American-born. Since the day of our naturalization, he had considered himself as American as any man who drew breath, made so by an act of the will and no longer obliged to former king and country. He shamed me, for I became an American with reservations, abjuring former loyalties with reluctance.

Nervous energy carried him, and when it flagged, he grew morose and suspicious of his friends.

"Edward is talking against me," he said, "he doesn't want me to win. He thinks I would neglect the store, which, of course, I would not do. And Amalie—at the lodge meetings the brothers break off their talk when I come in. What am I supposed to make of that?"

"It's concern. They can see how tired and overwrought you are. Please—you've done enough campaigning. Leave it to fate now."

He put his shaking hands to his head. "Must Stig beat on every kettle in the kitchen?"

"He's practicing for the election day parade, but I'll tell him to wait until you've gone."

In the kitchen Kamille was conducting Stig's rhythmic efforts with a ruler. She put it down with a sigh as Stig dropped his soupspoon drumstick.

"I hope Papa hurries and gets over politics," she said, as if office-seeking were a disease. Maybe it was, at that.

Peter was taking his hat from the hall tree to begin another evening of door-to-door campaigning.

"What can you tell people about yourself that they don't know already?" I protested.

"I must work to the end!"

"There's a chill in the air. Take your coat."

"No, if I do, I'll just leave it somewhere." He waved and went out, them came back through the door to kiss me good-bye.

"Sit down and count to ten before you go again," I urged, "it's bad luck if you don't!"

"Such foolishness, Amalie!" he laughed and was gone.

Hours later, he stumbled into the house and called for coffee. It had been raining, and his clothes were sodden. The skin under them felt like damp marble. I helped him strip and wrapped him in a quilt.

His eyes were hectically bright and his teeth chattered as he said, "It went better tonight."

We had kept no *snaps* in the house since we became aware of the prohibition of our church, so I tried to warm him with a mixture of hot water, honey, and lemon juice. I pulled a flat-iron to the front burner of the stove, and when it had heated through, wrapped it in a towel to warm his feet in bed. Nothing seemed to warm him, least of all my body. My pregnancy and his overpowering chill made us into two balls touching minimally.

In the early hours of the morning, I woke, burned by the heat of his skin.

"My chest, Amalie," he gasped, then coughed with a tearing sound.

Reaching for the matches to light the lamp, I knocked the box to the floor. My groping hands found a loose match, but there was no surface rough enough to strike it. Cursing myself for refusing electricity, I crawled under the bed, felt for a rough slat, and nearly set the mattress afire as the sulphur tip exploded into flame.

The first thing I saw was the blood-streaked sputum on the sheet. As I ran to the telephone to crank the night operator up from her pallet beside the switchboard, the unborn child thrashed in my body as if alarmed.

The sound of Doctor Gus's carriage clattering over the bricks of the silent streets woke the neighbors, and single lights came on here and there like answers to my cry for help.

It was pneumonia. Doctor Gus warned me to expect delirium and told me that someone must be with Peter night and day through the crisis ten days away.

"Right up to election day!" I said bitterly.

"He'd better win this one first," Doctor Gus said, clasping my shoulder, "you'll have to have some help with him."

"I can manage."

"I wish I had a pill for pride. Good night, Amalie."

Are the words of delirium a true cry of the heart? I preferred to think not when Peter called out Jonna's name, but when he murmured "Amalie," I thought it must be so. I sat beside his bed night and day, except for the few hours when exhaustion forced me to abdicate the watch to Valborg. He must have quantities of liquid, food, and rest, but he would have none of them, and I fought like a valkyrie to open his lips and teeth. He did not know me or understand the desperate love that drove me to this force. I was the enemy.

Morphine alone could give him the rest he must have. Doctor Gus gave me a packet of the powder to be dissolved in water and administered at the longest possible intervals. I pinned the package inside my apron pocket to keep it safe from the younger children, and when Peter's violent thrashing increased, speeding his painfully rasping breath, the morphine seemed to burn me through my clothes, offering itself before it was safe for him to have it.

I longed for sleep almost as intensely as I longed for Peter's improvement. I lusted for it, imagined my body stretched out to receive it, but I could not yield. I seemed to be walking in deep water to the accompaniment of a dull ringing.

When Peter had been ill for a week, three of his lodge brothers came to call. They saw how it was with me and offered to take turns sitting with him through the nights.

Frederick Clark was the first. He was a tall, spare man with a baldness patterned like a monk's tonsure. He handled Peter with a gentle firmness, ignoring the abuse of a man not in possession of himself. I slept soundly during Clark's watch.

During Abner Hardy's night, I was in and out of the room many times. Abner fumbled at his watch chain constantly, fixing his close-set eyes on Peter as he mumbled, "It's a terrible thing—a terrible thing!" When Peter tossed and cursed, Abner backed all the way to the windows as if he expected to be harmed.

"Go home, Abner," I said, "I'll manage."

"Oh no, Mrs. Jorgen, I'm only too glad to help! Do—do you think maybe you could give him some of that stuff now?"

"No, it's too soon."

On the third night I entrusted the morphine packet to Will Broder, who promised to hold off its use as long as humanly possible. Broder was the unofficial jester of the brotherhood, a fat, red-faced fellow who didn't hesitate to offer himself as the butt of a joke. He had the worst audience of his life that night, but his compulsive monologue kept him too busy to wonder whether he should resort to the morphine packet on the dresser.

On the day of crisis, Doctor Gus arrived early to examine Peter with a carefully noncommittal expression.

"Today or tonight we'll know," he said, "no morphine at all from here on in."

The day was a bad one. I was glad that the older children were in school and that Lily had taken Stig to her house. Peter moaned, coughed with a sound like tearing muslin, shouted at imaginary intruders, made political speeches, and cried heart-breakingly for his "Mor." The packet of morphine lay on the dresser, offering itself, but it was forbidden, and there would be no relief for me until the lodge brothers returned. All three of them meant to sit with Peter on this crucial night.

The children were home now, and I took them into the parlor to feed on their young prayers and offer my own. Before going to bed, I looked in on Peter, holding his tossing head to kiss him on the lips in spite of three onlookers.

I was awakened by drums and the blare of cornets. Election day. Easing from the bed without waking Valborg, I put on my wrapper and hurried to the sick room. The door was shut and no sound came from inside. I opened it carefully. Clark slumped sideways in a chair beside the bed, asleep. Will Broder snored on the floor, his head pillowed on a bent arm, and Abner Hardy was in another chair, his chin on his chest and his hands folded over his watch chain. Peter was neatly covered, his head turned in profile on the pillow. The flush of fever was gone from a face that might have been carved from ivory.

"Thank God!" I cried.

The lodge brothers woke at the sound of my voice, hawking and yawning as they tried to shake the stiffness from their limbs.

Abner Hardy was brushing his hair before the dresser mirror when I screamed. The silver-backed brush dropped from his hand as I lunged for the half-empty morphine packet. "You've killed him!"

"We couldn't let it go on—"said Frederick Clark, whom I'd

trusted; "we gave him just enough to let him sleep—Jesus Christ Himself wouldn't have kept it from him!" He quickly herded the others out of the room, closing the door gently.

"Four went to sleep," I said to the emptiness, "three woke up. Sleep—sleep—" I pulled the covers back from Peter's cold hands, thinking to kiss them, but with his spirit gone out of him, they were only things, objects. I covered them again and looked long at his face. There was no light in it now, and I, who had lived for so long in its light, must grope in darkness. The candle stolen from our wedding feast was Peter's, and I had no wish to burn on like the one that was left.

The morphine. Was it enough to take me where Peter had gone? The water pitcher was empty, and I went to the kitchen pump. As I was pouring a dipper of water down the pump to prime its flow, Kamille's bare feet kissed the cold floor behind me.

"'Morning, Mama," she yawned.

Automatically I said, "Where are your slippers? You'll catch cold!"

The child I had forgotten I carried leaped in my body as if to say, "I want to live!" I carried the morphine packet to the stove and watched my escape go up in flames. Then I woke the other children and told them that their father was dead.

All through that dreadful day the cornets blared and the drums pounded. When their mockery was stilled, Lily Hertert came to tell me that Peter would have been the mayor of Harlan had he lived.

"*Tak for Alt!*" I said bitterly.

Lily looked at me with gentle puzzlement.

I shook my head and shifted in my chair to ease the heaviness in my body. There was much that Peter should have known before he left us.

When Lily went home, I sat at my kitchen table and prayed.

"I give up, God, I will never understand Your ways. Do what You can with me in spite of that."

Peter was buried from the Christian Church, for I knew this would be his wish. I also knew that he would understand my need to go back to the Lutherans and take comfort from the "Kyrie" and the Danish sermons.

On the twenty-ninth day of December, I cranked the telephone to call Doctor Gus, and Petra was born a few hours later. Since the worst had happened to me, I had no fear and named her for the dearest of my dead.

As Petra's life began, I took up my own again. Its colors were drabber, its sounds more muted, and its tastes more bland, but I accepted my minor resurrection gladly and took pleasure in the curl of Petra's tiny fist and her blind clinging to the breasts that she alone could invest with importance now.

I was a well-to-do widow of thirty-five who held the respect of the community. My children needed me, and I would live out my life for them. All my fires were banked.

24

I stayed in the house the whole of that winter. The older girls did the necessary shopping and Stig took care of Holger, who was growing fat and torpid in his stall in the carriage house. Stig begged to ride him, but I would not allow it.

My days were taken up by the care of Petra, rubbing oil into the furniture, tending my house plants, and cooking all the dishes Mor used to make.

Much virtue attached to visiting widows and orphans in their affliction, and my front door opened daily to the curious and the truly sympathetic. I found the former easier to bear, for I could make a game of withholding the things they wanted to know.

"What will happen to the Beehive?" Mrs. Nicolai asked.

"What has always happened, I suppose."

"You mean you will retain your interest in it?"

"*Det bliver min sag,*" I replied with a shrug, and Mrs. Nicolai didn't dare to press for the translation—"That's my affair."

"Mr. Nicolai told me to ask if you would like to sell Holger," she said; "we'd like to help in any way we can."

"Thank you, but I will keep Holger. He is a friend."

"Well, since you sold the carriage horses, I thought you might be in need—"

I smiled enigmatically.

"Well," she sniffed, "it's nice that you can afford to be so independent. You do have five children to raise, you know."

"I know," I said, smiling at Petra asleep in her longskirted basket.

The visit was cut short by the return of Valborg and Else from an ice-skating party on the Nishnabotna. Their cheeks were red as Graasten apples, and they wore their skates into the kitchen, having found a run of ice all the way from the river to our house.

"They'll cut up your floors!" Mrs. Nicolai gasped.

"They'll be off again as soon as they're warm," I said indulgently, "it's a lot of bother to unstrap."

Mrs. Nicolai went off shaking her head and I was left to muse about the alteration in my house pride. Now I kept up the other rooms better than I ever had done, but the kitchen was the room where we lived, and there were no rules or restrictions there. Anyone who was sick reclined on a daybed along the south wall. A big, hinged chest held the toys of the younger children. My set of Dickens was stacked in a corner against the day when I might take enough interest in human experience to read again.

Just now, it was enough to watch the sun's rays bend through the wavy glass of the windows and listen to the shrill voice of the teakettle pulled to the front burner for the company of its whistle. Once the first racking grief was past, life without Peter was a plateau of uneventful existence. I seldom knew what day it was, and when the children turned a leaf of the calendar to a new month, I was without regret or anticipation.

Until they begged me to put their long underwear away, I had no notion that spring had come. I stepped into the yard to test the temperature and saw the young grape leaves uncurling on the vines of the arbor. The breeze carried the bittersweet scent of the prairie's greening.

"You may change to muslin," I said, leaving the back door ajar as I came in.

With wild whoops they ran to their rooms to shed the cumbersome, baggy garments that had imprisoned them for months. When I next saw them, they were slimmer and more graceful—butterflies freed from the essential but ugly chrysalis. The change forced me to look at them more carefully than I had for months.

Valborg had ripened, not to beauty, but to a healthy attractiveness. She was in love for what would be the first of many times. I should have listened more carefully when she told me about the boy, because I searched for his name and could not find it.

Else had grown vain—with cause. She loved chiefly herself, and the sheer arrogance of that regard forced unwilling admiration from others.

Kamille was all eyes and angles, a dreamer who gave common things the lustre of imagination. She was forever telling Stig about Papa's activities in heaven, inventing a house for Peter, angel friends, and a business of selling the goods for celestial robes. One would think she had been dipping into my Swedenborg, but that could not be. Turned against it by Lily, I had packed the book away in the crawl space above the trap door in our bedroom.

And there was Stig, so often willful and stubborn, just coming into the years when a boy needs a man to imitate. I had let him run with companions I did not know all winter, and the spring blooming of my neglect was filthy language and small cruelties, which he brought home in all innocence. That innocence disarmed me, and I reproved but did not punish. Stig was so beguiling in easy repentance.

"Stay in the yard, Stig," I said as the three girls went off to school.

"Can't I go to Lily's?" he begged.

"Well, just for a little while."

Petra was crowing and kicking in the beechwood cradle. She had outgrown the fancy, skirted basket that had been the gift of Lily and John.

"What will you be?" I asked, smiling into her elfish little face. She laughed out loud.

As I went about opening the windows to spring, I felt the restlessness of long confinement for the first time. I had been so much with my children that I could no longer see them clearly. It was time to walk out of this house, if only for a little while.

I bundled Petra into a shawl and crossed the street to Lily's back door. Stig was enjoying a stack of cookies and a glass of milk at Lily's kitchen table, and he did not seem pleased at the prospect of sharing his Lady Bountiful.

On sudden impulse, I said, "Lily, will you take care of these two for a little while? I think I'll saddle Holger and ride."

"That's a marvelous idea!" she said, reaching for Petra, "I was beginning to wonder if you would ever come out of it."

I'm not sure I want to—it's comfortable to be numb—but spring won't let me stay that way. The children are out of their union suits, and well. . ."I shrugged, laughing.

Holger puffed his sides and wheezed a complaint as I cinched him tightly. I had rejected my own sidesaddle for Peter's, but I could not pull the strap to the well-worn notch he had used. Holger was fatter and I was weaker. This was just one more instance of being unable to take Peter's place, but I would try, riding astride in his saddle.

A stray dog was enough to make Holger shy after a long, cozy idleness in his stall, and I took the quickest route out of town.

The prairie, which once bordered our first house by the mill, had given way to cultivated land. I saw farmers walking behind the steel self-scouring plows that made the breaking of the prairie possible. The black-brown earth parted before the blade, falling away like scoops of hand-cranked ice cream. Something in my Jutland heart rejoiced at the cultivation, but something new and possibly American yearned for prairie untouched by man. I rode far enough to find it and urged Holger to a wild gallop through tall grasses, dead and brown at the level where they brushed my saddle-divided skirt, but green far below, where spring was working its miracle.

Whipped from his lethargy, Holger was exhilarated by that great, free space, and he tried to shake the bit from his teeth when I turned him back toward town.

"We're only free for a little while," I said, leaning forward to slap him on the neck affectionately.

As I rode back into town on Sixth street, I passed Edward Parmeter in his one-seater. He seemed surprised to see me and stared pointedly at my unsuitable dress and saddle.

"May I call tomorrow?" he asked.

"Of course." After I said it, I wished I hadn't, but my reluctance to see Edward was ridiculous. After all, he had handled all the business matters after Peter's death, and I should be grateful to him.

When Edward arrived, I was waiting in a black broadcloth dress too heavy for the weather. The breeze that billowed the parlor curtains was languorously warm, and I cooled myself with the Spanish fan Far had given me on my confirmation day.

"Are you speaking to me in the language of the fan,

Amalie?'' he asked.

This was the first time he had used my given name, and both the address and the question flustered me.

"I doubt that such language is of use in talking business," I answered, folding the fan.

"Something must be done about the partnership, of course, but perhaps we can come to a solution that will embrace more than business. By the way, is your clutch of children likely to pop from behind the settee? I had hoped for a private conversation."

"You shall have it," I said curtly, refusing to volunteer the fact that we were alone in the house. I sat down on the settee and straightened my back primly, folding my hands in my black lap.

"I hadn't meant to speak to you so soon," he said, "but when I saw you out riding like a hoyden, I realized I had misjudged your sense of the niceties."

"How can you talk to me that way?" I cried, amazed at my degree of hurt. I had experienced no feeling so sharp in more than half a year.

"I'm sorry," he said, taking my hand, "that was harsh, but your reaction told me what I needed to know. You do feel something for me."

"No! It's shocking that you should—"

His lips were hard on mine. The hands I raised to push him away seemed to have a will of their own, spreading to press his chest and shoulder in passionate exploration. I could not think. It was like the time with Birch Sandahl in the wood. I could not break from Edward, and when he released me, I turned from him, horrified at myself.

"Please go, I am ashamed!"

"You needn't be. Nothing stands in our way now."

"But I don't like you, Edward!" I said between clenched

teeth, "I never have!"

"Liking is for friends," he said. "We are something else."

"Buy Peter's share in the Beehive from me and leave me alone!"

"I can't. Since Peter died, business has fallen off, and I don't have the money."

"Borrow it from John Hertert," I said, frightened by the implications of what he had told me.

"Be sensible, Amalie; the obvious solution to the whole problem is for us to marry, though I confess that I can't quite see myself as a paterfamilias."

"Get out!" I screamed, sickened by the impossible longing for him that survived even this cold-blooded proposition.

He stood and took his hat from the cane-seated chair that had been my mother's. "Madame, I apologize. I deeply regret your attitude, for aside from the financial soundness of my plan, I had looked forward to possessing you."

"*Slange!*" I shouted, too agitated to use English.

He bowed, smiled, and left me, not knowing that I had called him a snake.

Snake! Snake! Snake! The word rang with the echo of the front door's slamming. A snake on the misty Danish heath, a snake in the musty dampness of the root cellar on the farm, a snake that had entered and left this house with coil and thrust.

Birch Sandahl, Berg Landsman, Edward Parmeter. Why did my mind group them? I paced, pressing my clasped hands hard against my breastbone, shaking my head in a horrified denial of a question that demanded an answer.

"Oh, God, don't let the children come home yet!" I said aloud, and the sound of my voice frightened me. I went to the kitchen and tried to make a pot of coffee, but my hands shook too fiercely to measure and pour.

The question was written on the walls, on the shaft of afternoon sun that slanted through the window, on the pickets of the fence around the house.

What am I?

"Mor! Mother!" The cry burst from me with all the anguish of the moment of death, and I sat back drained, no longer fighting the question or its answer.

I saw my mother. Bodil and a faceless pastor walked on the heath, and as they went deeper into the moor, I felt the coursing of her blood, the mindless power that had moved my hands over Edward Parmeter's shoulders.

I had blamed her for succumbing to that power, for being deafened to the whisper of conscience by the roar of her blood; blamed her and buried the deed so deep that I never expected to think of it again.

No one would ever know how close I had come to yielding to Edward. If a widow of thirty-five, with six living children, could feel such engulfing temptation, what of a girl of sixteen?

I knew her now as I never had known her before, and it was too late to tell her so. My blood was her blood; a bequest not to be despised, for it had been my gift to Peter—the first helping of my heart.

My hands stopped shaking, and I made the coffee.

John Hertert took over my business affairs; at Lily's insistence, I suspected. I had no need to see Edward, but when a few months had passed, I was strong enough to walk into the Beehive, greet him, and make a purchase. I knew myself now, and his gaze no longer had the power to confound me.

I came home to find the younger children playing dominoes at the kitchen table. When they clamored for my old fairy tale, "Amalie's Story," I told it. "But you must remember," I said, "the story isn't true."

"We know, Mama," Kamille said, "but we like it anyhow."